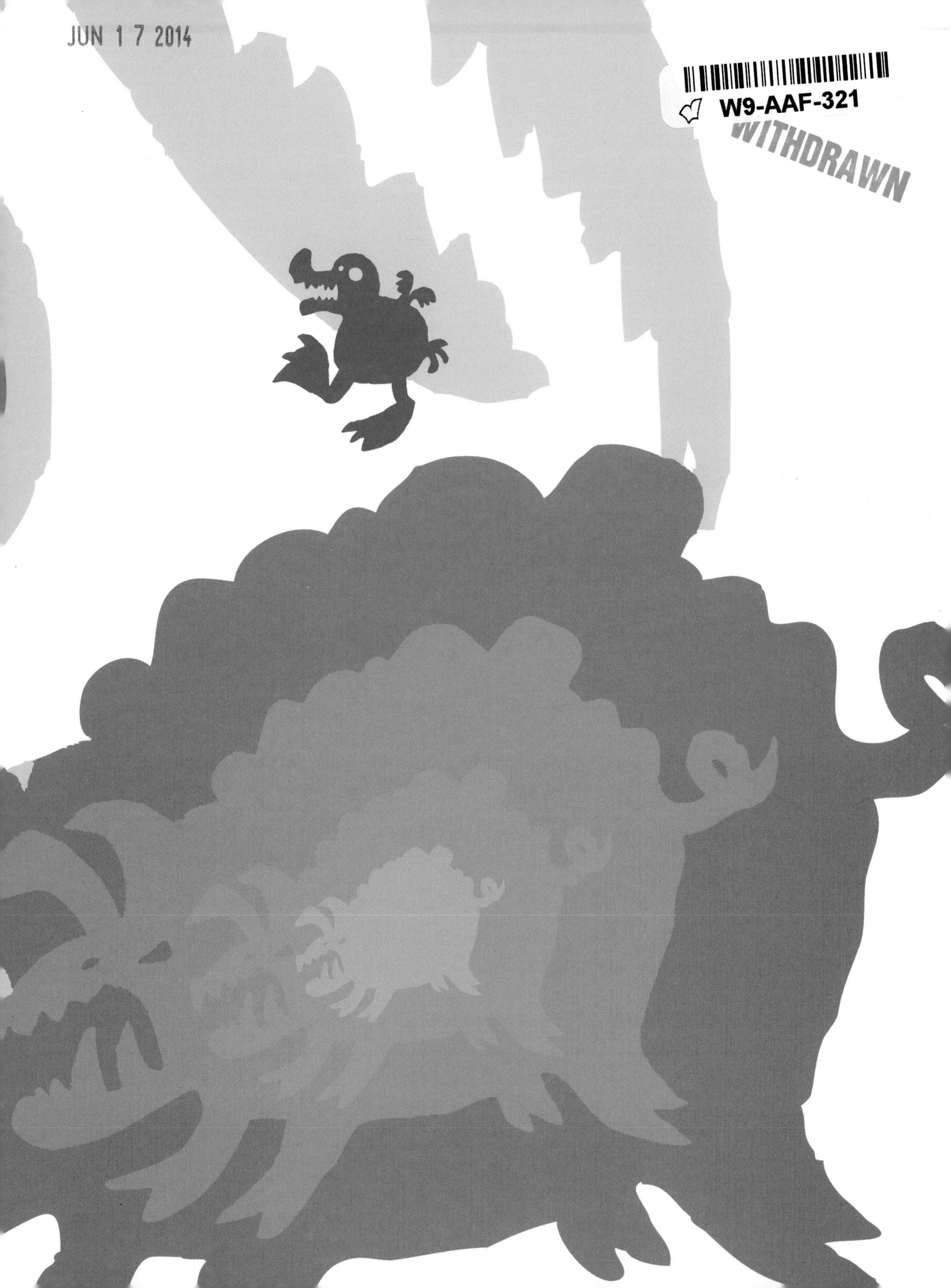

Lewis Trondheim

Monster Turkey

Jean   Dad   Kriss   Petey   Mom

PAPERCUTZ ™

New York

IMPORTANT! READ THIS FIRST!

Petey and Jean love to draw pictures of monsters. One day they draw a scary monster that comes alive—it escapes right off the paper and disappears into their home! Well, they certainly have to do something about that, so they drew a nice monster, with three legs, four arms, and ten mouths to eat the bad monster. The plan works and Petey and Jean decide to keep the nice monster as a pet... and they name it Kriss.

Monster GRAPHIC NOVELS AVAILABLE FROM PAPERCUTZ ™

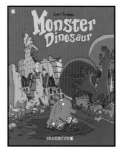

"Monster Christmas" $9.99
(hardcover only)

"Monster Mess" $9.99
(hardcover only)

"Monster Dinosaur" $9.99
(hardcover only)

"Monster Turkey" $9.99
(hardcover only)

MONSTER #4 "Monster Turkey"
Originally published as
Monster Dindon, volume 3, Lewis Trondheim
Copyright © 2000 Guy Delcourt Productions.
All rights reserved. English Translation Copyright
© 2012 by Papercutz. All rights reserved.

Lewis Trondheim — Story, Art, & Color
Joe Johnson — Translation
Michael Petranek — Lettering
Janice Chiang — Logo
Adam Grano — Production
Michael Petranek — Associate Editor
Jim Salicrup
Editor-in-Chief

ISBN: 978-1-59707-349-3

Printed in China
October 2012 by New Era Printing LTD.
Trend Centre, 29-31 Cheung Lee St.
Rm.1101-1103, 11/F
Chaiwan, Hong Kong

Papercutz graphic novels are available at booksellers everywhere. Or order from us: Please add $4.00 for postage and handling for the first book, add $1.00 for each additional book.

Please make check payable to
NBM Publishing

Send to:
PAPERCUTZ, 160 Broadway, Suite 700, East Wing,
New York, NY 10038 (1-800-886-1223)

WWW.PAPERCUTZ.COM

DISTRIBUTED BY MACMILLAN
FIRST PAPERCUTZ PRINTING

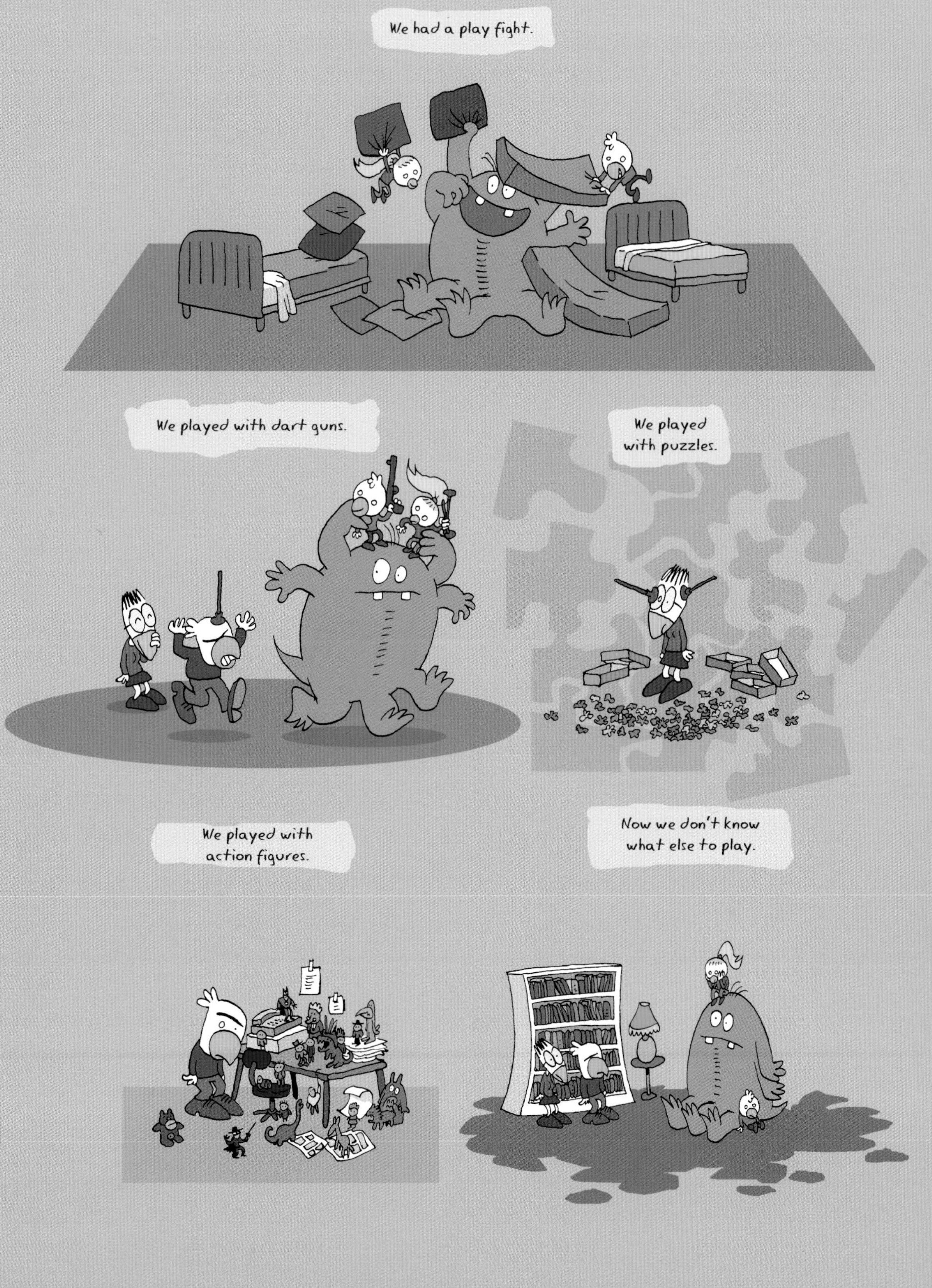
We had a play fight.
We played with dart guns.
We played with puzzles.
We played with action figures.
Now we don't know what else to play.

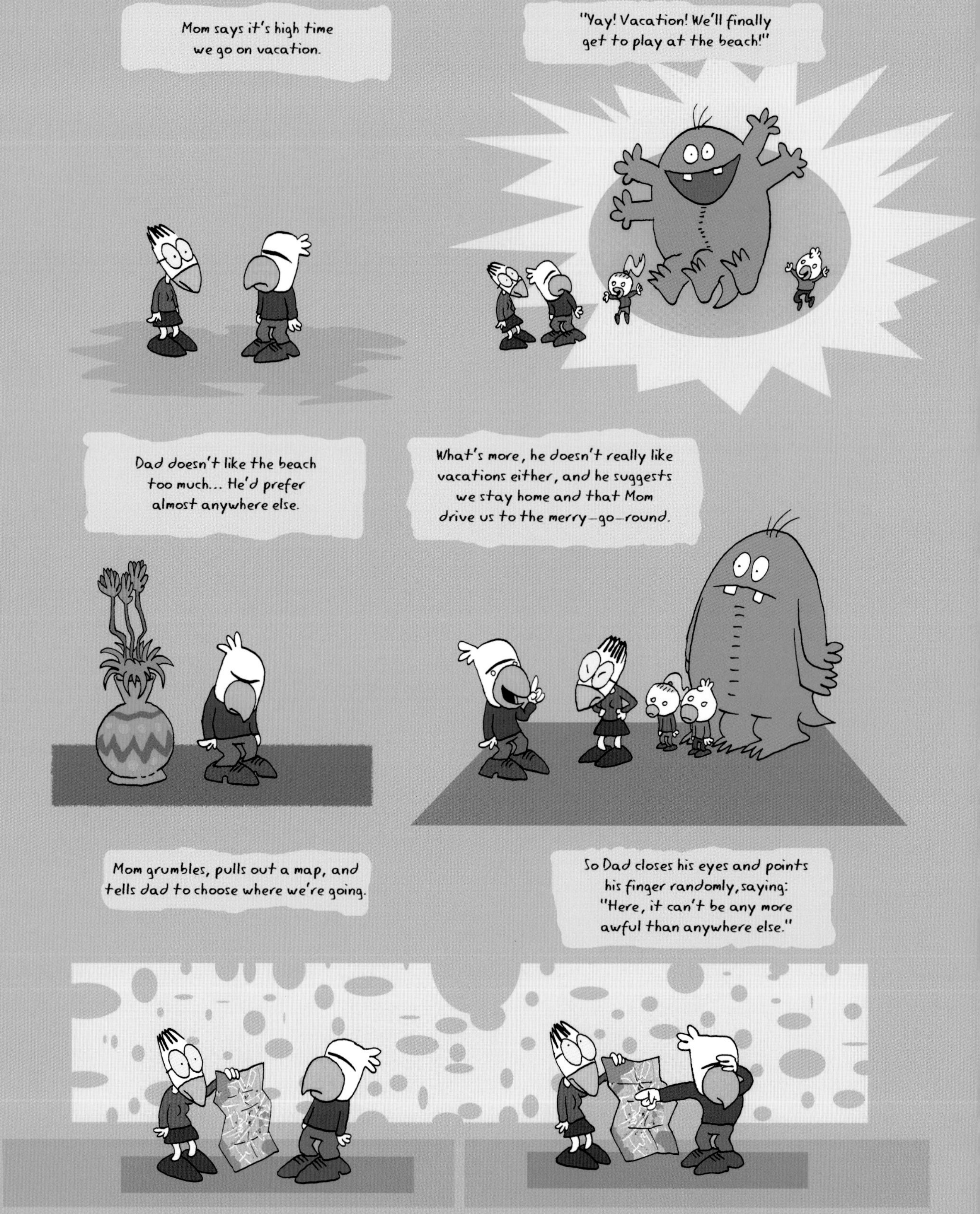
Mom says it's high time we go on vacation.
"Yay! Vacation! We'll finally get to play at the beach!"
Dad doesn't like the beach too much... He'd prefer almost anywhere else.
What's more, he doesn't really like vacations either, and he suggests we stay home and that Mom drive us to the merry-go-round.
Mom grumbles, pulls out a map, and tells dad to choose where we're going.
So Dad closes his eyes and points his finger randomly, saying: "Here, it can't be any more awful than anywhere else."

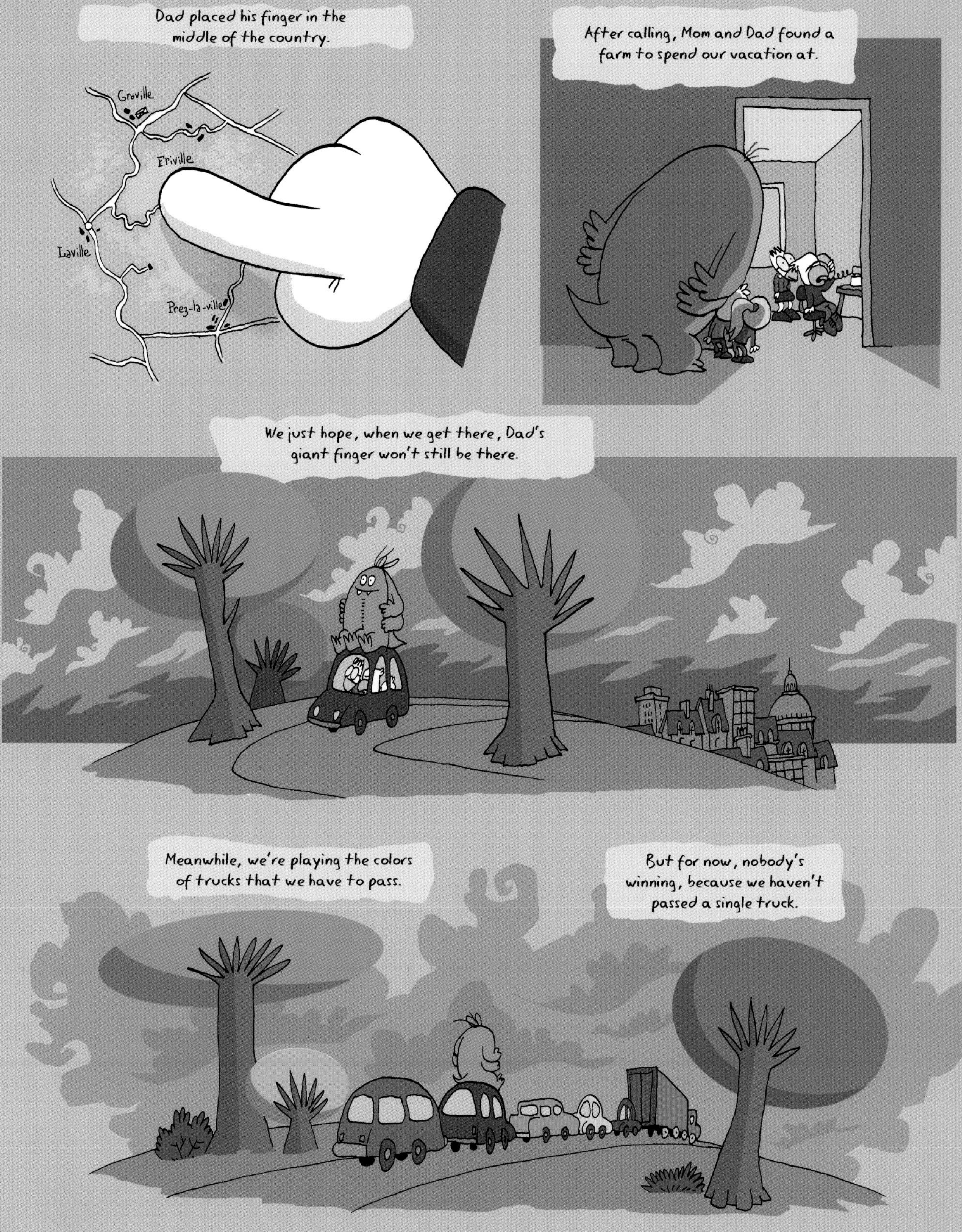
Dad placed his finger in the middle of the country.
Groville
Friville
Laville
Prez-la-ville
After calling, Mom and Dad found a farm to spend our vacation at.
We just hope, when we get there, Dad's giant finger won't still be there.
Meanwhile, we're playing the colors of trucks that we have to pass.
But for now, nobody's winning, because we haven't passed a single truck.

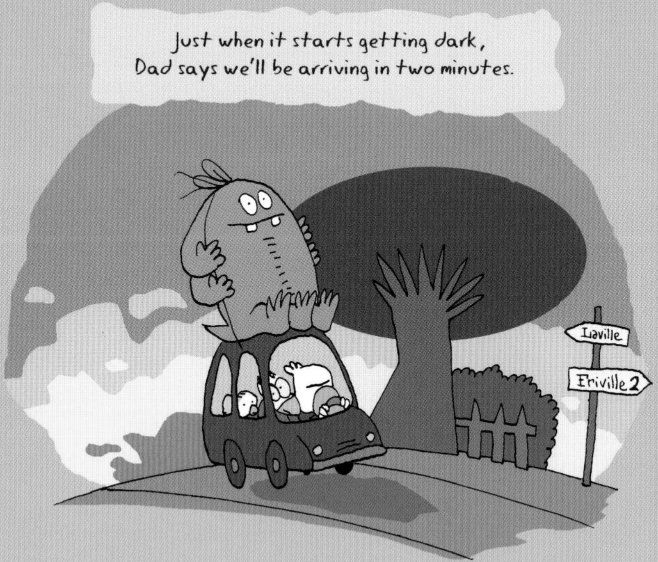
Just when it starts getting dark, Dad says we'll be arriving in two minutes.
Liaville
Eriville 2

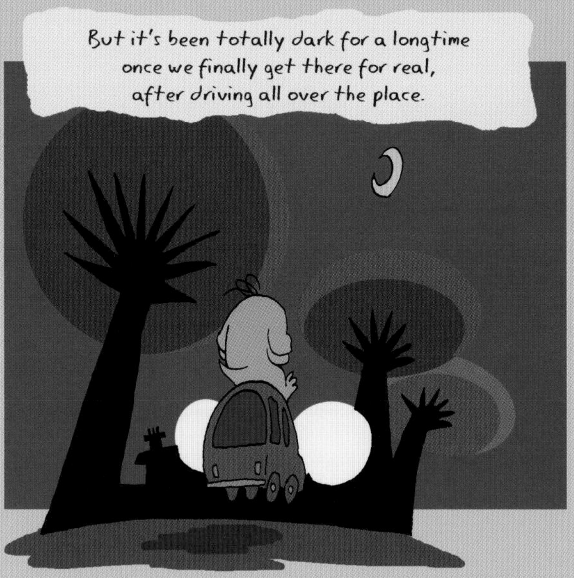
But it's been totally dark for a longtime once we finally get there for real, after driving all over the place.

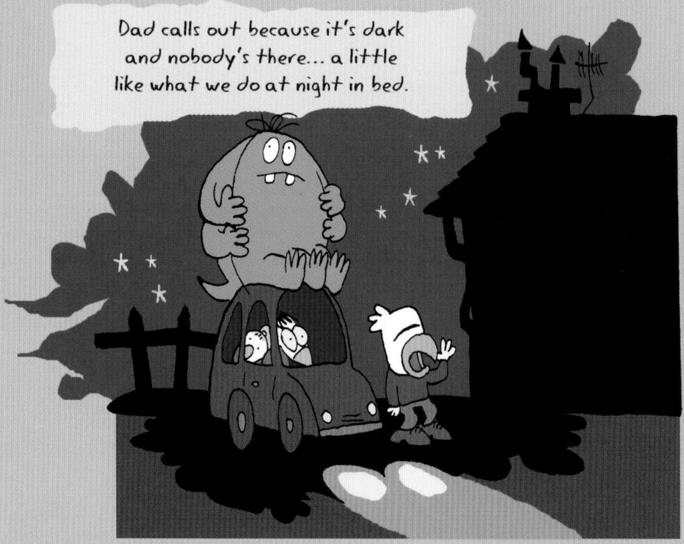
Dad calls out because it's dark and nobody's there... a little like what we do at night in bed.

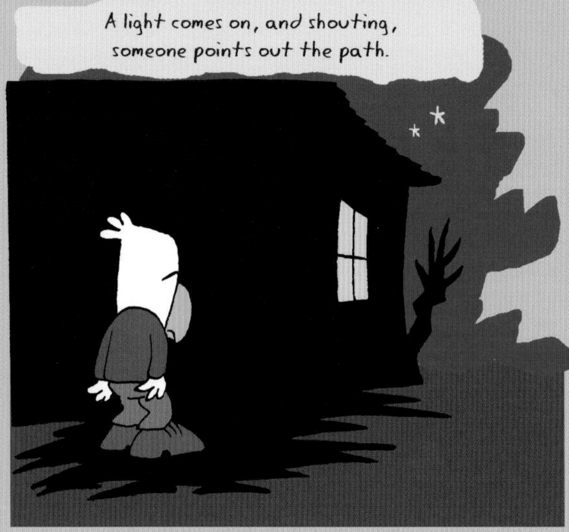
A light comes on, and shouting, someone points out the path.

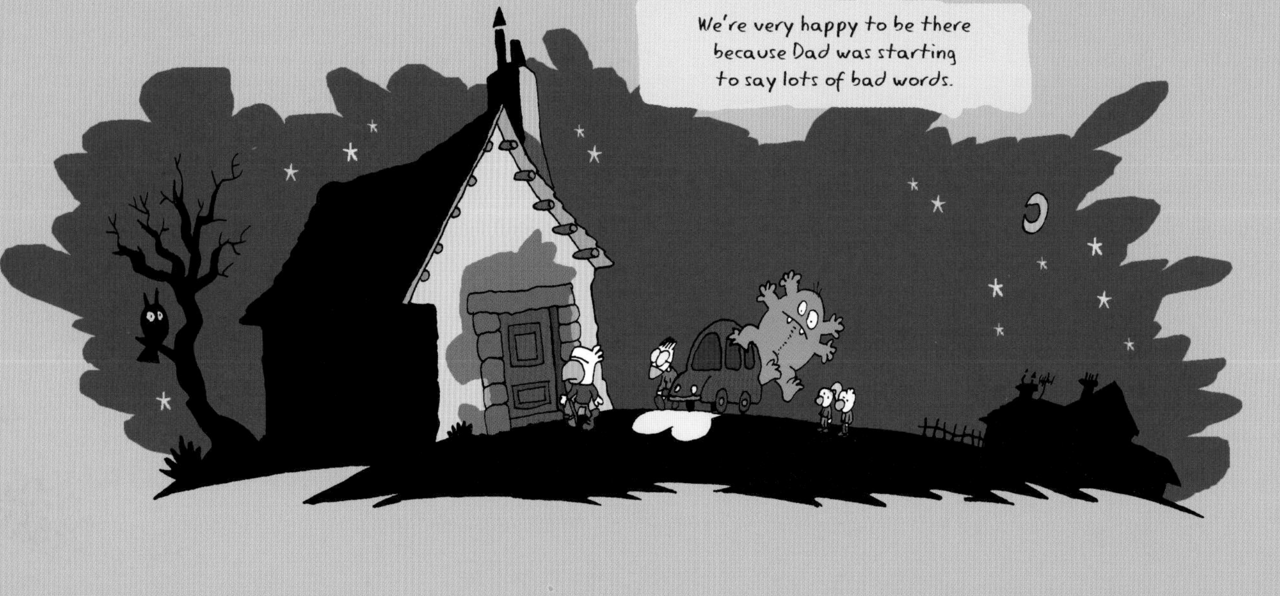
We're very happy to be there because Dad was starting to say lots of bad words.

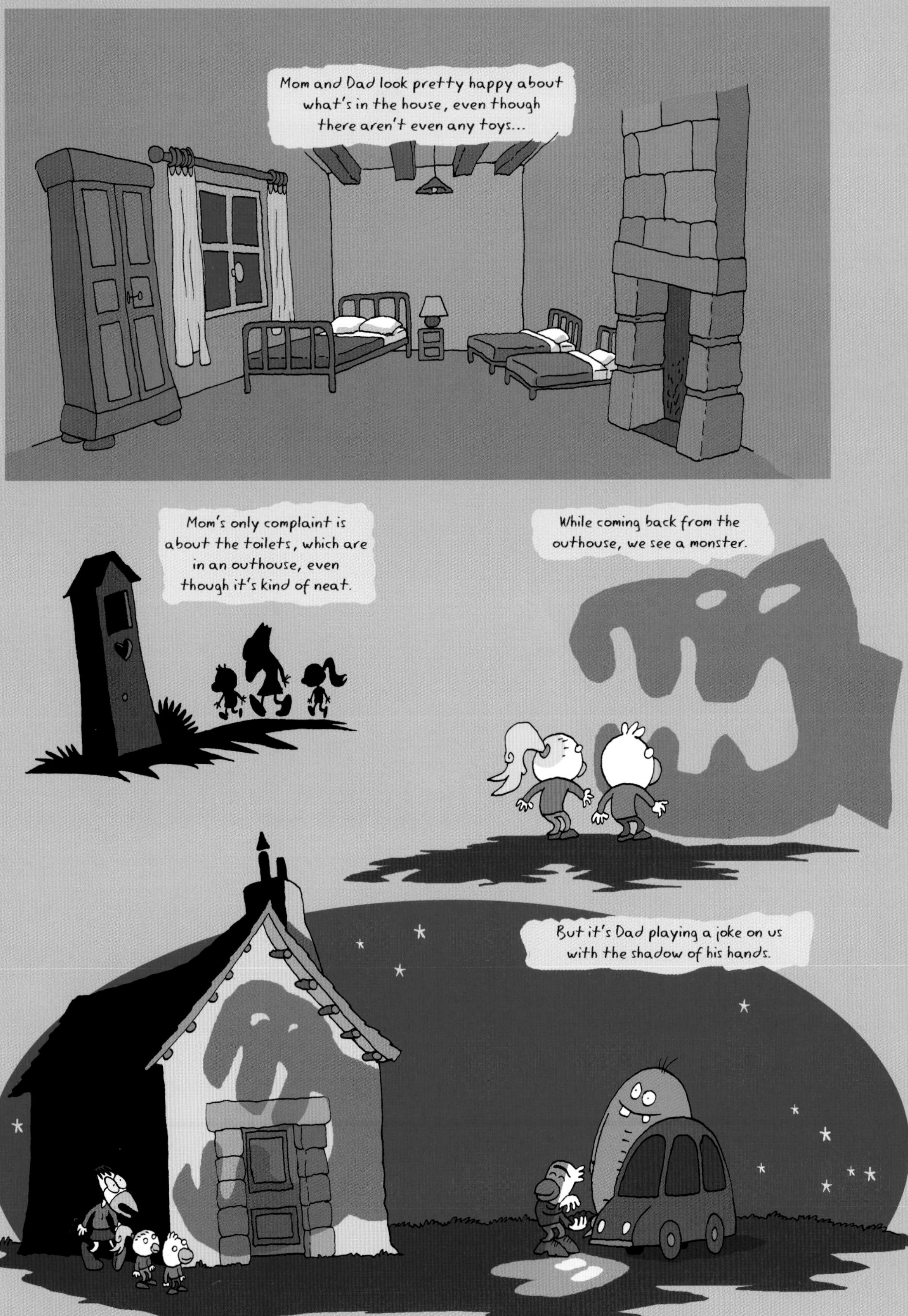
Mom and Dad look pretty happy about what's in the house, even though there aren't even any toys...
Mom's only complaint is about the toilets, which are in an outhouse, even though it's kind of neat.
While coming back from the outhouse, we see a monster.
But it's Dad playing a joke on us with the shadow of his hands.

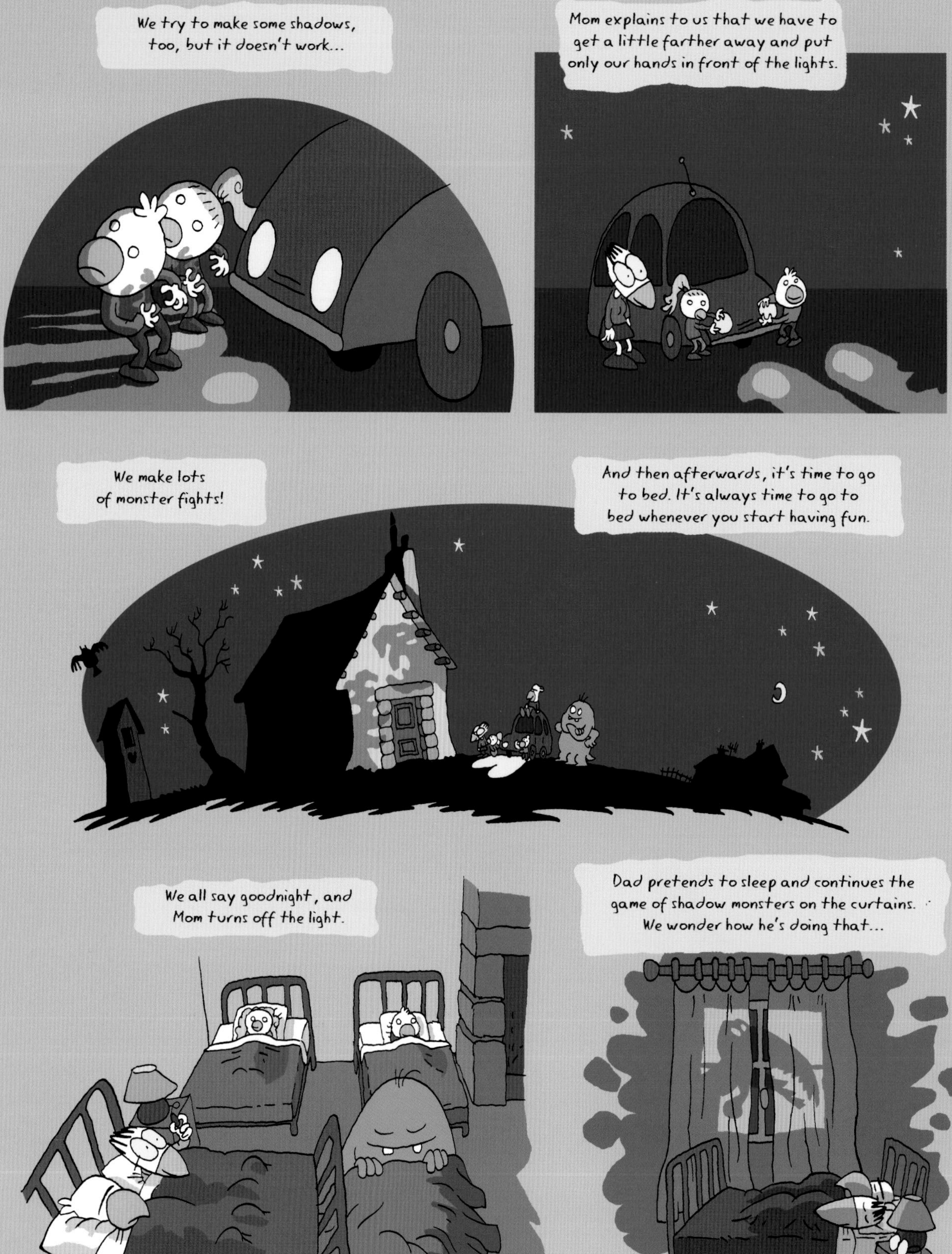
We try to make some shadows, too, but it doesn't work...
Mom explains to us that we have to get a little farther away and put only our hands in front of the lights.
We make lots of monster fights!
And then afterwards, it's time to go to bed. It's always time to go to bed whenever you start having fun.
We all say goodnight, and Mom turns off the light.
Dad pretends to sleep and continues the game of shadow monsters on the curtains. We wonder how he's doing that...

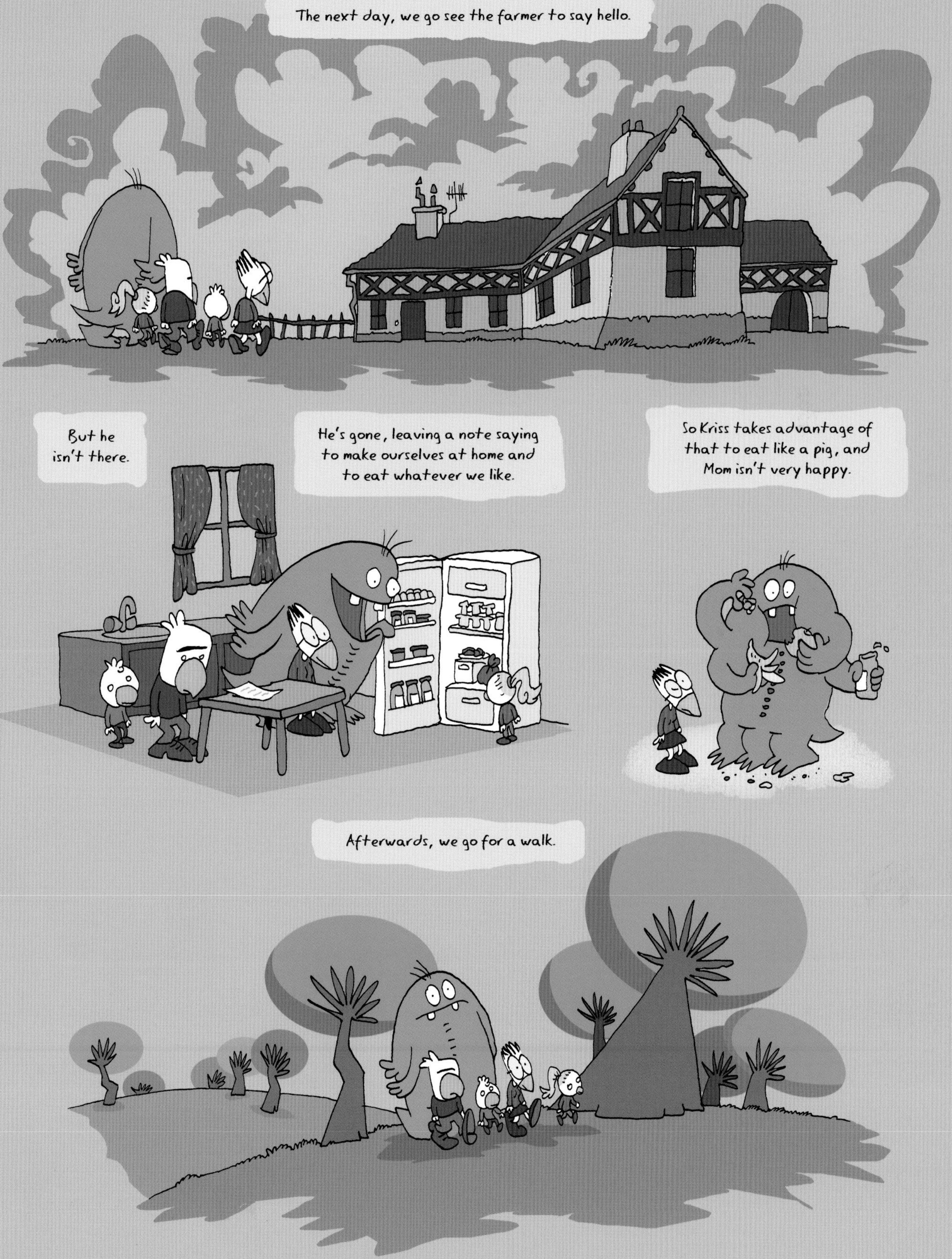
The next day, we go see the farmer to say hello.
But he isn't there.
He's gone, leaving a note saying to make ourselves at home and to eat whatever we like.
So Kriss takes advantage of that to eat like a pig, and Mom isn't very happy.
Afterwards, we go for a walk.

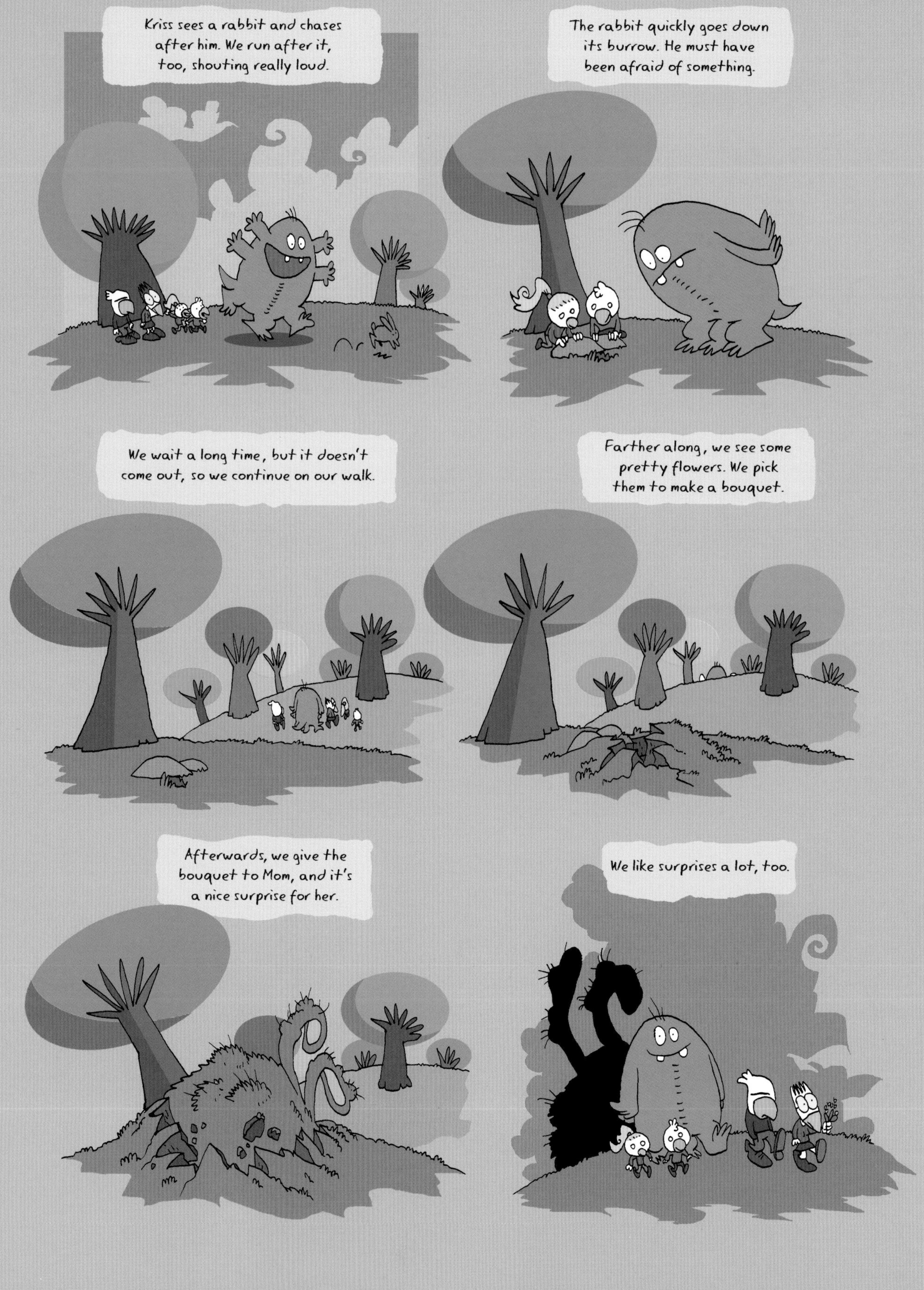
Kriss sees a rabbit and chases after him. We run after it, too, shouting really loud.
The rabbit quickly goes down its burrow. He must have been afraid of something.
We wait a long time, but it doesn't come out, so we continue on our walk.
Farther along, we see some pretty flowers. We pick them to make a bouquet.
Afterwards, we give the bouquet to Mom, and it's a nice surprise for her.
We like surprises a lot, too.

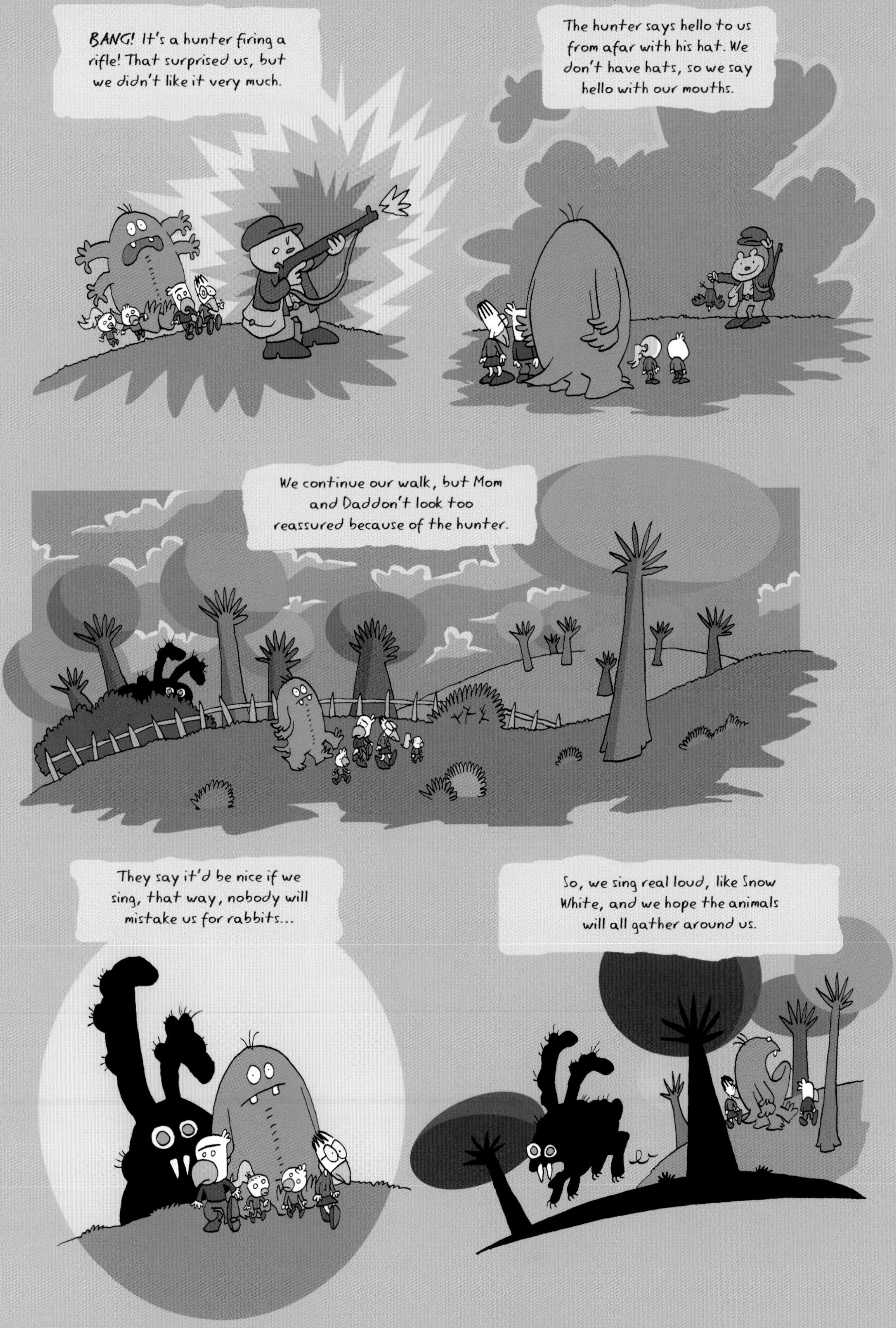
BANG! It's a hunter firing a rifle! That surprised us, but we didn't like it very much.
The hunter says hello to us from afar with his hat. We don't have hats, so we say hello with our mouths.
We continue our walk, but Mom and Daddon't look too reassured because of the hunter.
They say it'd be nice if we sing, that way, nobody will mistake us for rabbits...
So, we sing real loud, like Snow White, and we hope the animals will all gather around us.

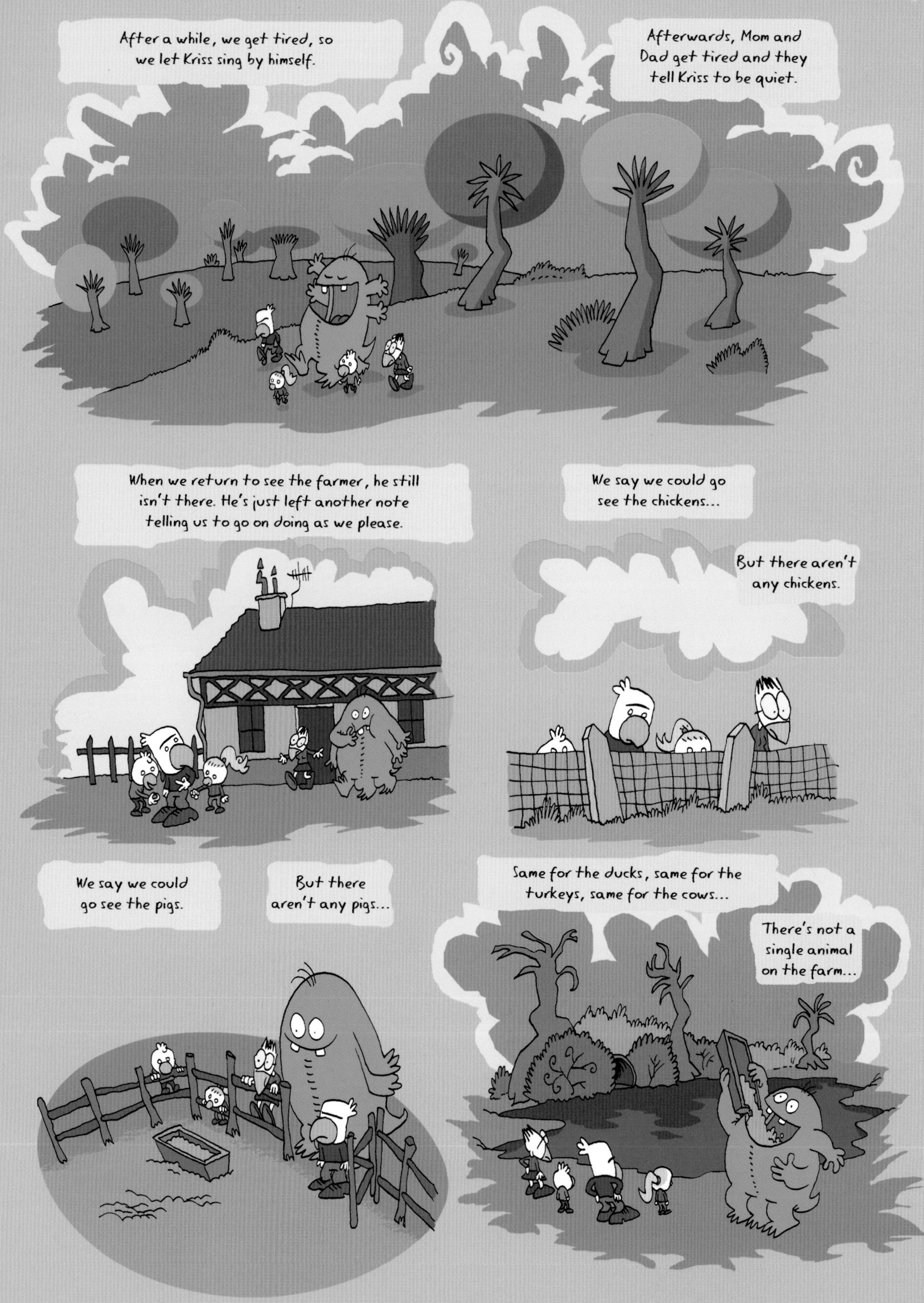
After a while, we get tired, so we let Kriss sing by himself.
Afterwards, Mom and Dad get tired and they tell Kriss to be quiet.
When we return to see the farmer, he still isn't there. He's just left another note telling us to go on doing as we please.
We say we could go see the chickens...
But there aren't any chickens.
We say we could go see the pigs.
But there aren't any pigs...
Same for the ducks, same for the turkeys, same for the cows...
There's not a single animal on the farm...

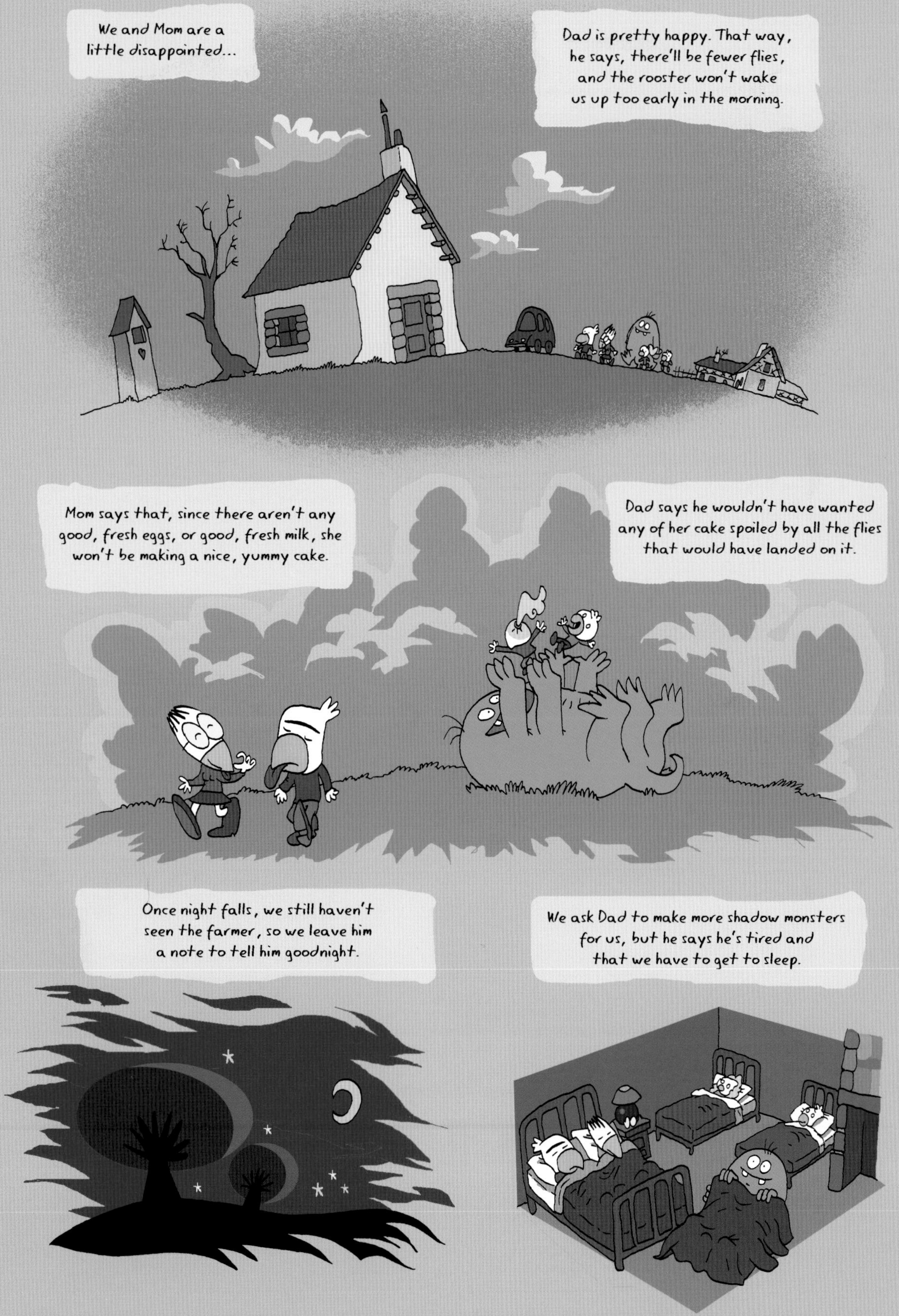
We and Mom are a little disappointed...
Dad is pretty happy. That way, he says, there'll be fewer flies, and the rooster won't wake us up too early in the morning.
Mom says that, since there aren't any good, fresh eggs, or good, fresh milk, she won't be making a nice, yummy cake.
Dad says he wouldn't have wanted any of her cake spoiled by all the flies that would have landed on it.
Once night falls, we still haven't seen the farmer, so we leave him a note to tell him goodnight.
We ask Dad to make more shadow monsters for us, but he says he's tired and that we have to get to sleep.

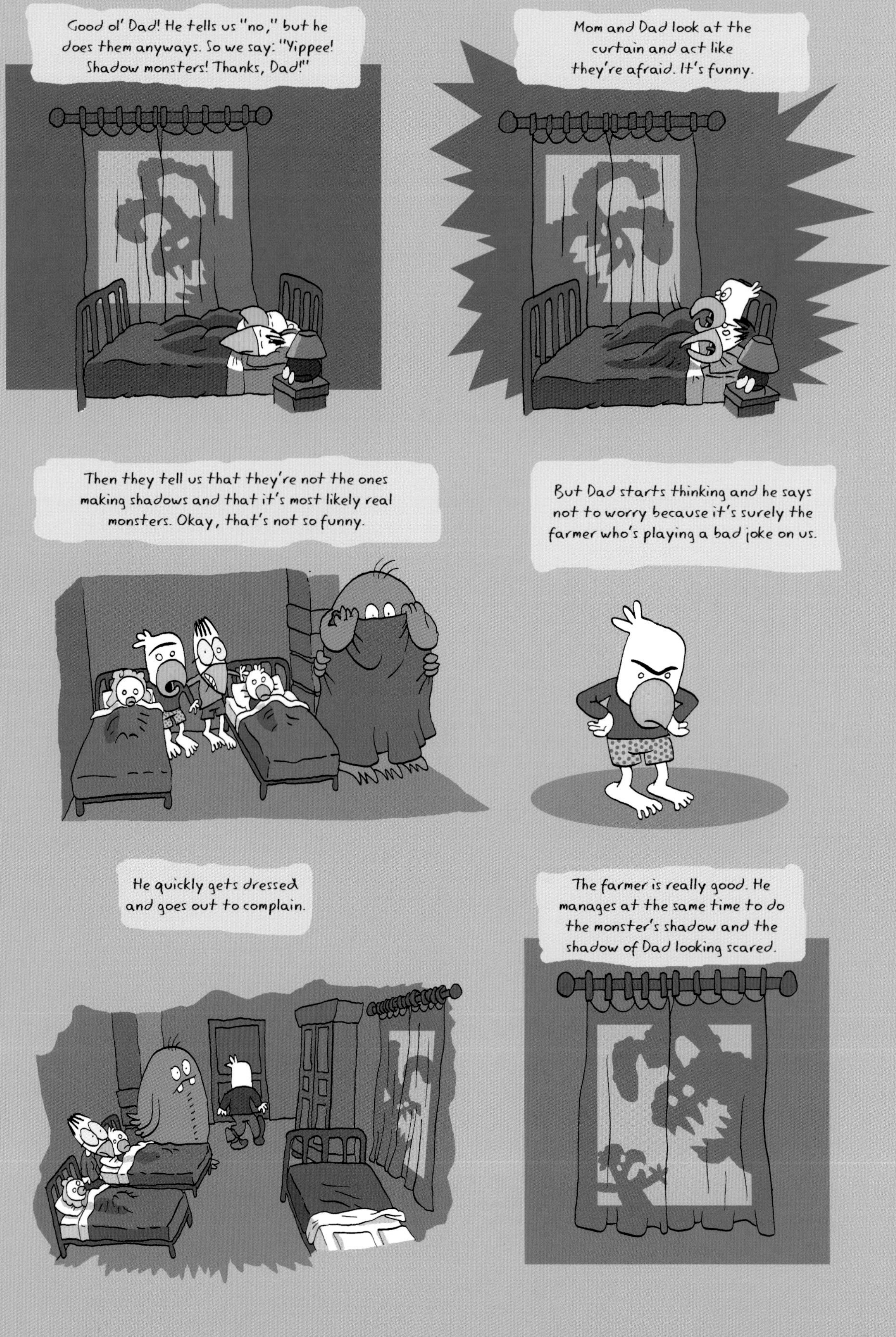
Good ol' Dad! He tells us "no," but he does them anyways. So we say: "Yippee! Shadow monsters! Thanks, Dad!"
Mom and Dad look at the curtain and act like they're afraid. It's funny.
Then they tell us that they're not the ones making shadows and that it's most likely real monsters. Okay, that's not so funny.
But Dad starts thinking and he says not to worry because it's surely the farmer who's playing a bad joke on us.
He quickly gets dressed and goes out to complain.
The farmer is really good. He manages at the same time to do the monster's shadow and the shadow of Dad looking scared.

And then the shadow of Dad running and screaming.

And the shadow of Dad falling.

Finally, Dad comes back and tells us to barricade the door because it's a real monster!

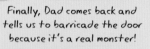

So, we push the armoire against the door so nobody can come in.

While we get dressed, Kriss and Dad also barricade the window.

Now that everything's barricaded, nobody else can get in.

We'd like to run away, but now we can't run away either.

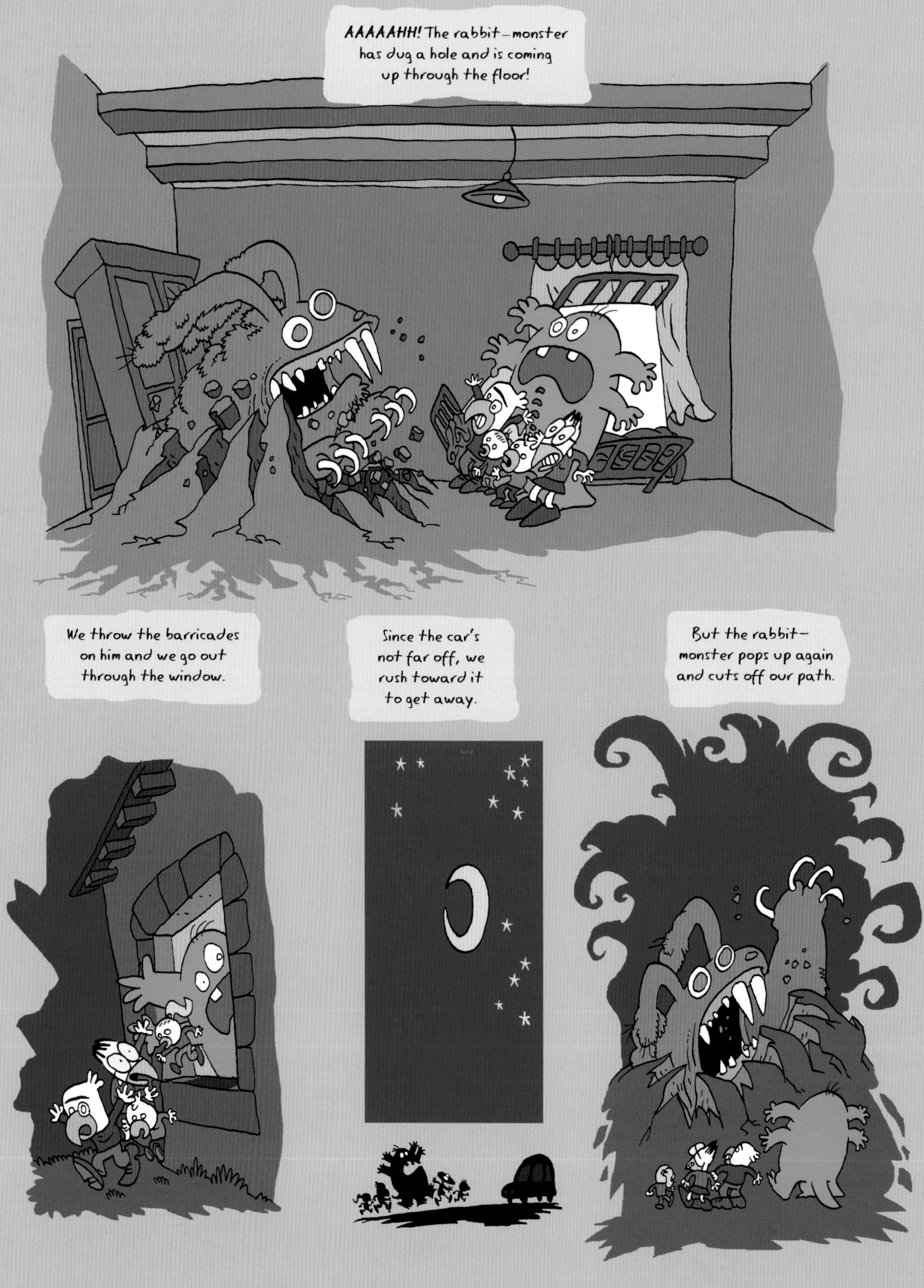
AAAAAHH! The rabbit-monster has dug a hole and is coming up through the floor!
We throw the barricades on him and we go out through the window.
Since the car's not far off, we rush toward it to get away.
But the rabbit-monster pops up again and cuts off our path.

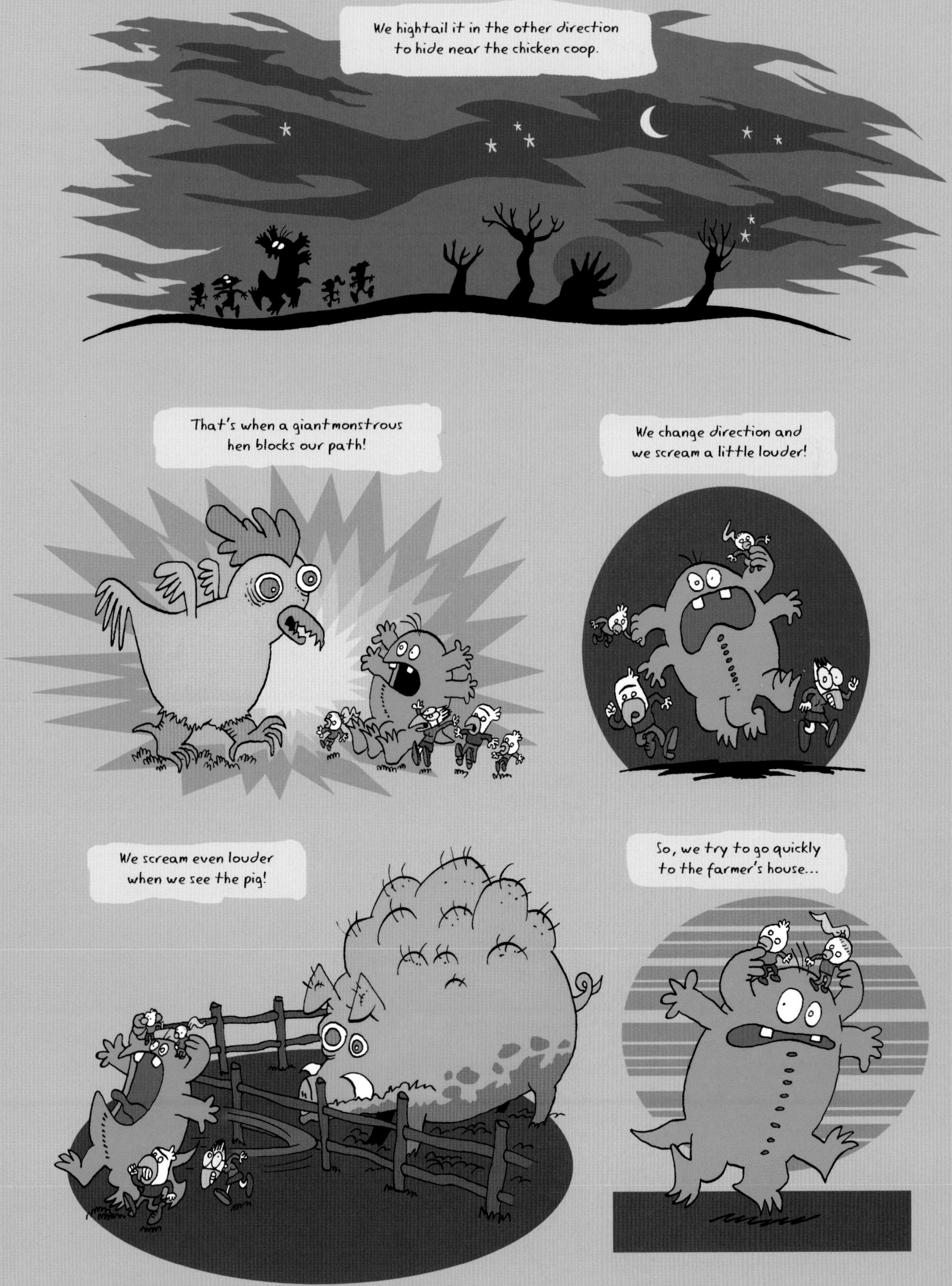
We hightail it in the other direction
to hide near the chicken coop.
That's when a giant monstrous
hen blocks our path!
We change direction and
we scream a little louder!
We scream even louder
when we see the pig!
So, we try to go quickly
to the farmer's house...

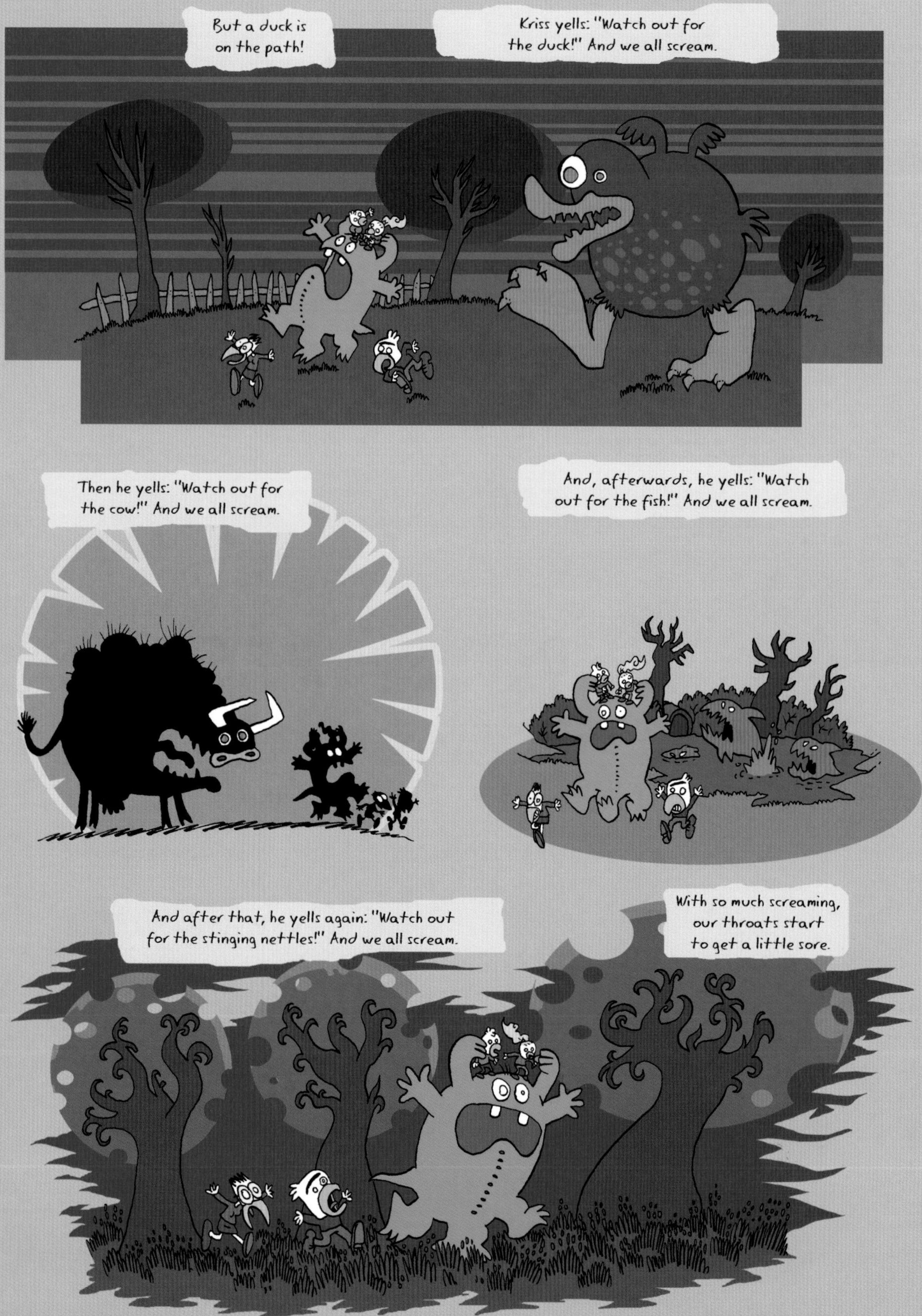
But a duck is on the path!
Kriss yells: "Watch out for the duck!" And we all scream.
Then he yells: "Watch out for the cow!" And we all scream.
And, afterwards, he yells: "Watch out for the fish!" And we all scream.
And after that, he yells again: "Watch out for the stinging nettles!" And we all scream.
With so much screaming, our throats start to get a little sore.

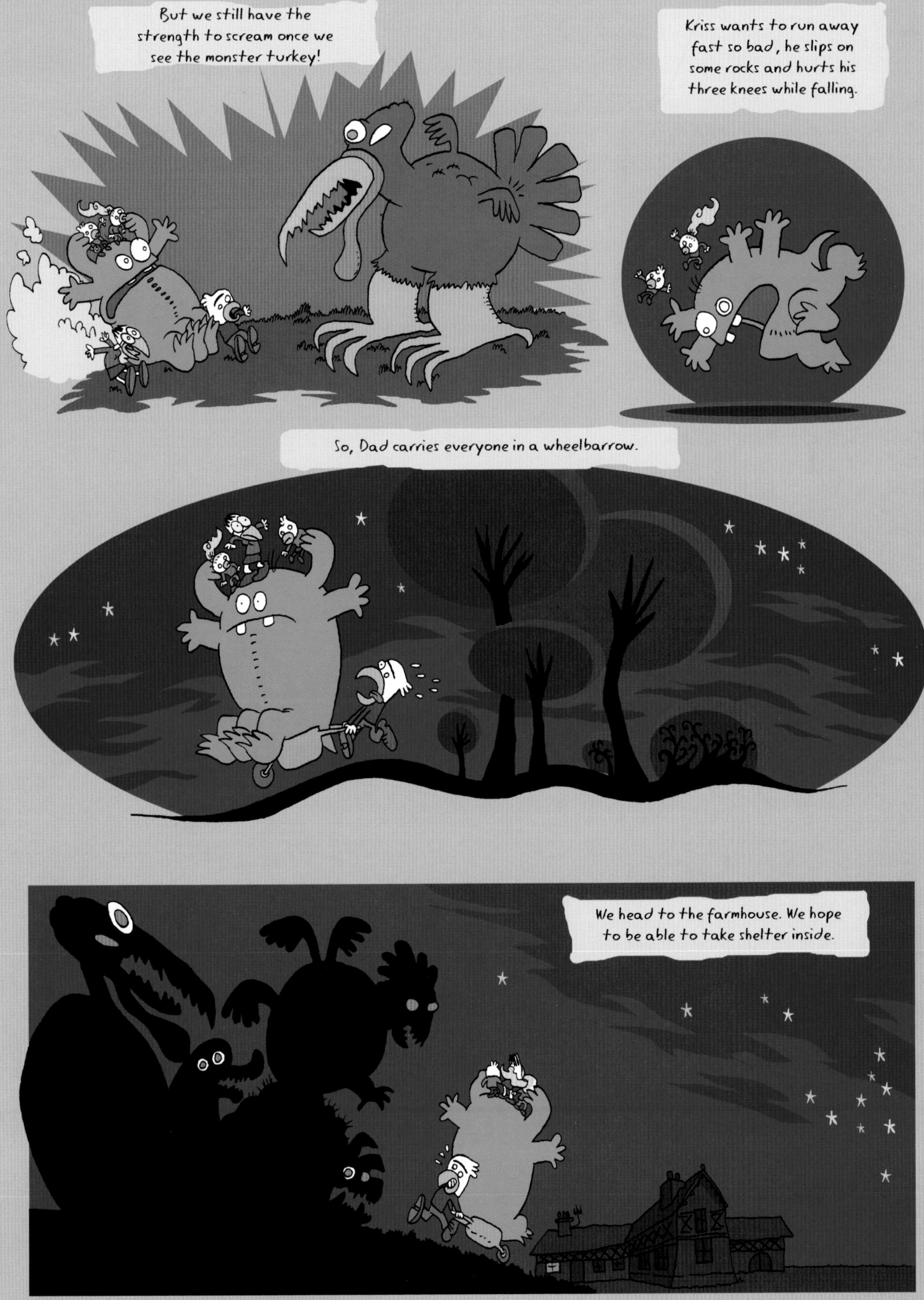
But we still have the strength to scream once we see the monster turkey!
Kriss wants to run away fast so bad, he slips on some rocks and hurts his three knees while falling.
So, Dad carries everyone in a wheelbarrow.
We head to the farmhouse. We hope to be able to take shelter inside.

Once Kriss sees the fridge, he can walk on his own again.

But Mom says now's no time for eating.

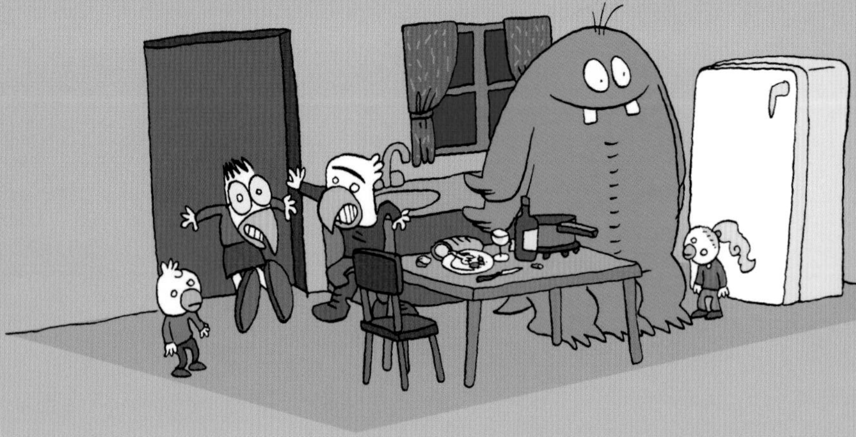

It's too bad because there's lots of good stuff on the table.

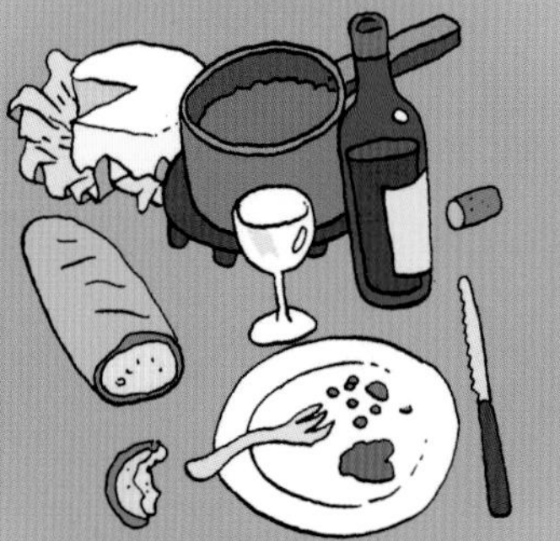

"The farmer must have seen the monsters and run away," says Dad.

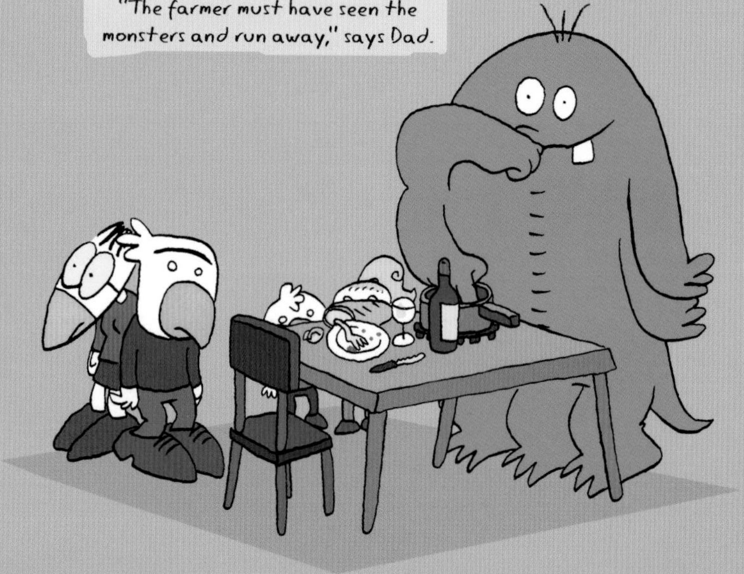

We say there are too many monsters for us to fight them and that the only real solution for getting rid of them is to call Batman and Zorro!

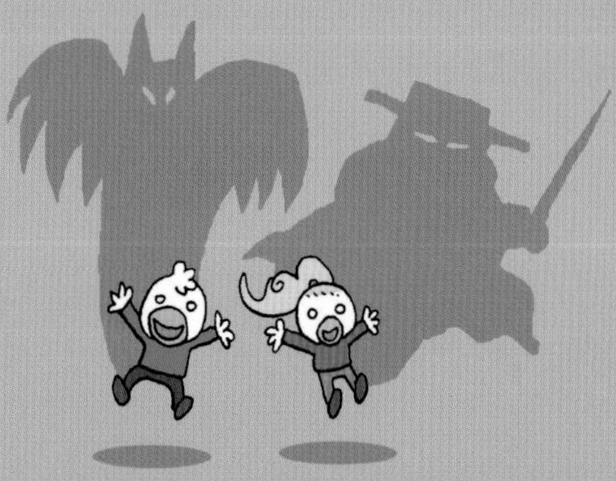

Dad thanks us for our good idea and he says he'll settle for just calling the police for the moment.

Except he can't find the phone.

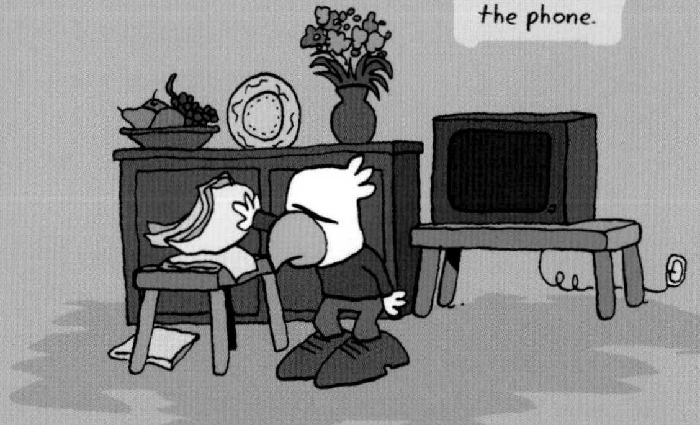

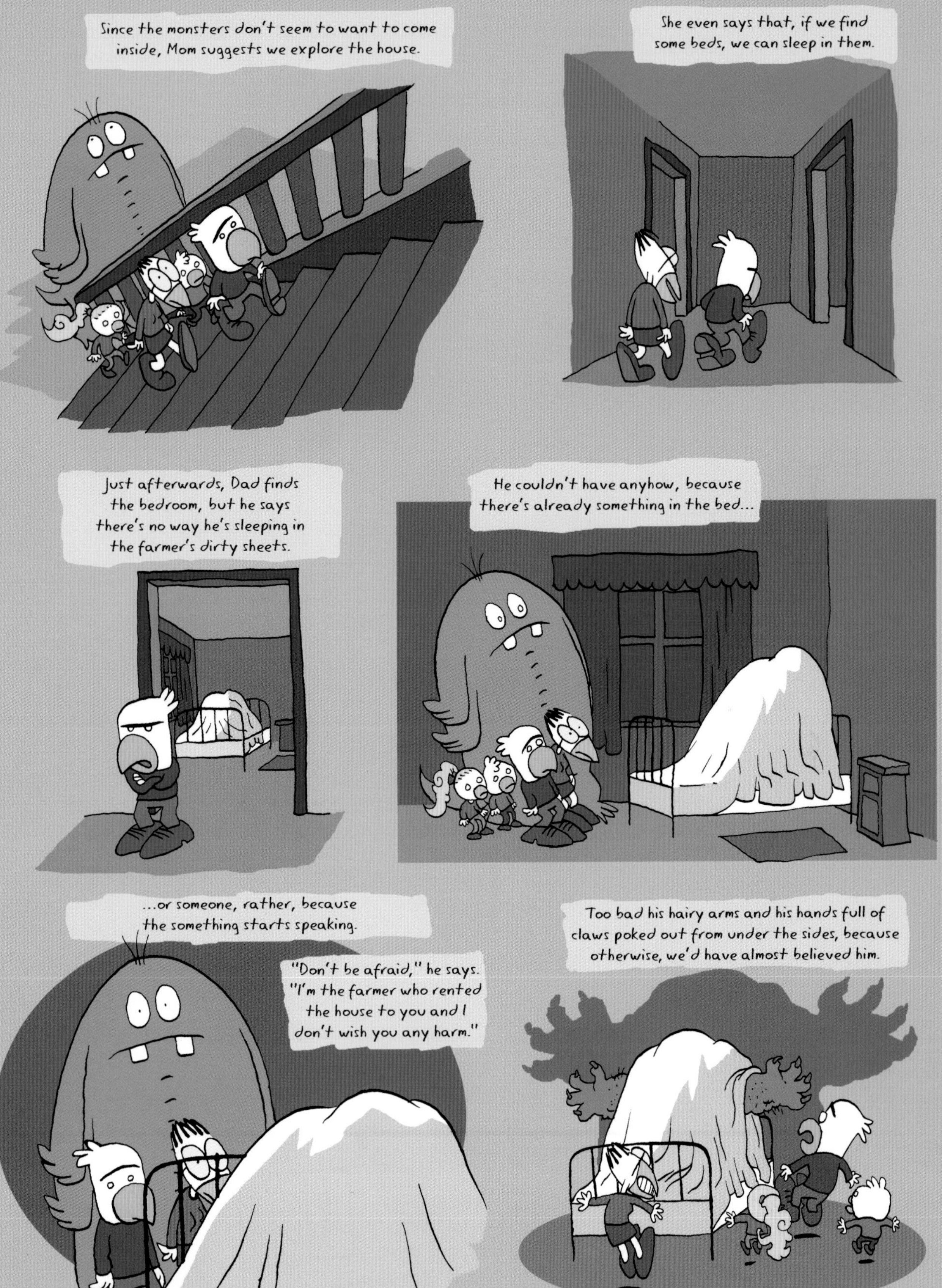

Since the monsters don't seem to want to come inside, Mom suggests we explore the house.
She even says that, if we find some beds, we can sleep in them.
Just afterwards, Dad finds the bedroom, but he says there's no way he's sleeping in the farmer's dirty sheets.
He couldn't have anyhow, because there's already something in the bed...
...or someone, rather, because the something starts speaking.
"Don't be afraid," he says. "I'm the farmer who rented the house to you and I don't wish you any harm."
Too bad his hairy arms and his hands full of claws poked out from under the sides, because otherwise, we'd have almost believed him.

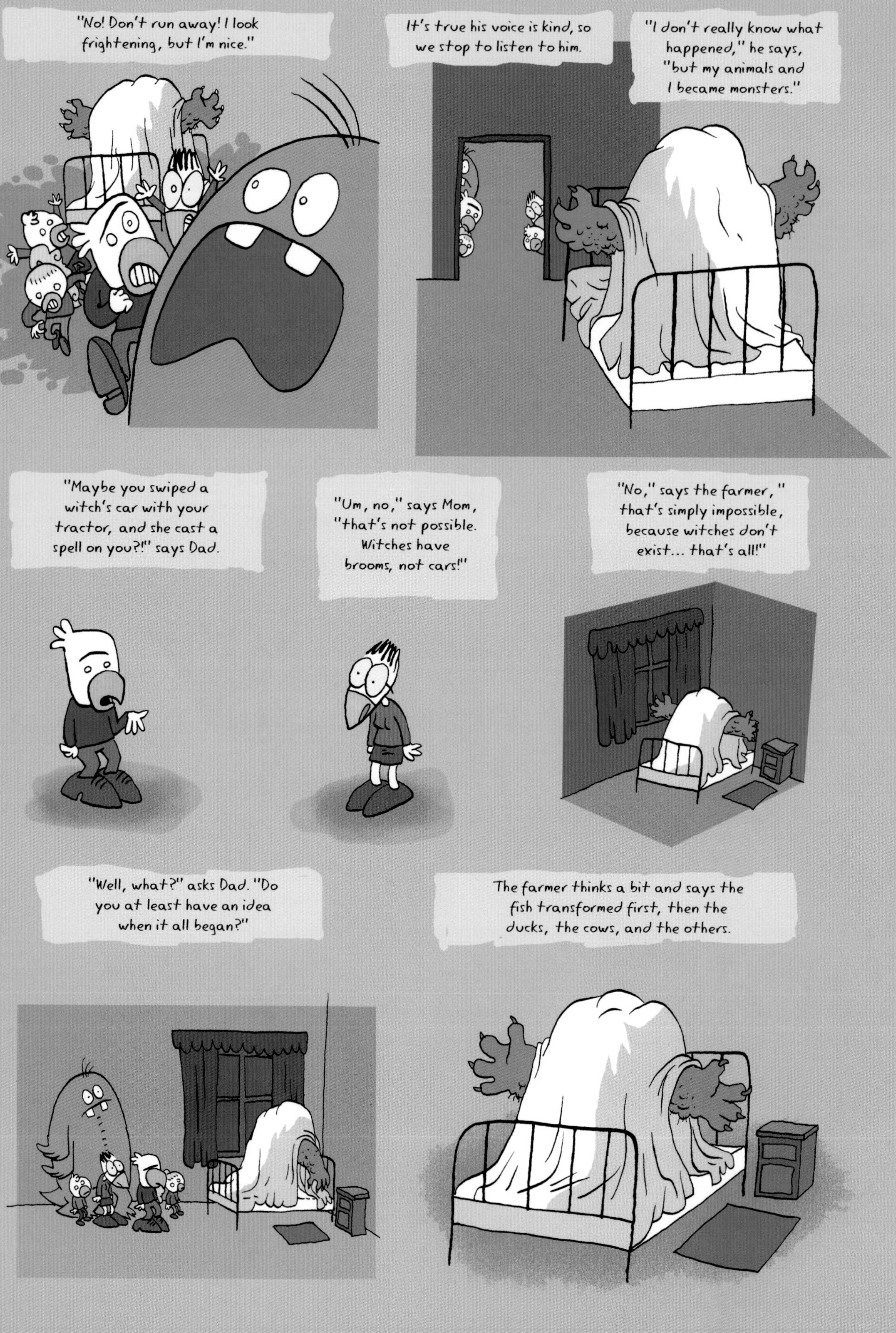
"No! Don't run away! I look frightening, but I'm nice."
It's true his voice is kind, so we stop to listen to him.
"I don't really know what happened," he says, "but my animals and I became monsters."
"Maybe you swiped a witch's car with your tractor, and she cast a spell on you?!" says Dad.
"Um, no," says Mom, "that's not possible. Witches have brooms, not cars!"
"No," says the farmer, " that's simply impossible, because witches don't exist... that's all!"
"Well, what?" asks Dad. "Do you at least have an idea when it all began?"
The farmer thinks a bit and says the fish transformed first, then the ducks, the cows, and the others.

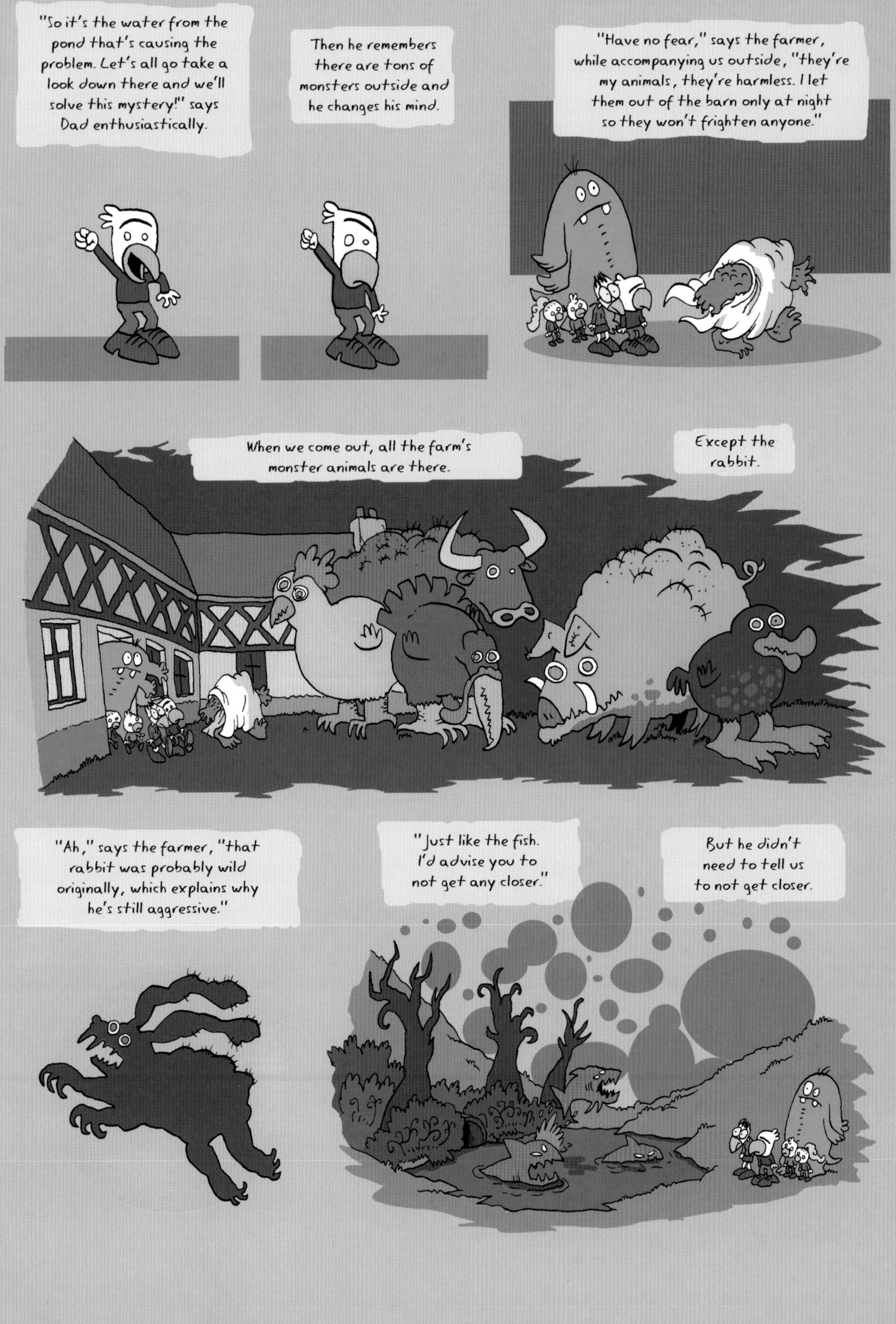
"So it's the water from the pond that's causing the problem. Let's all go take a look down there and we'll solve this mystery!" says Dad enthusiastically.
Then he remembers there are tons of monsters outside and he changes his mind.
"Have no fear," says the farmer, while accompanying us outside, "they're my animals, they're harmless. I let them out of the barn only at night so they won't frighten anyone."
When we come out, all the farm's monster animals are there.
Except the rabbit.
"Ah," says the farmer, "that rabbit was probably wild originally, which explains why he's still aggressive."
"Just like the fish. I'd advise you to not get any closer."
But he didn't need to tell us to not get closer.

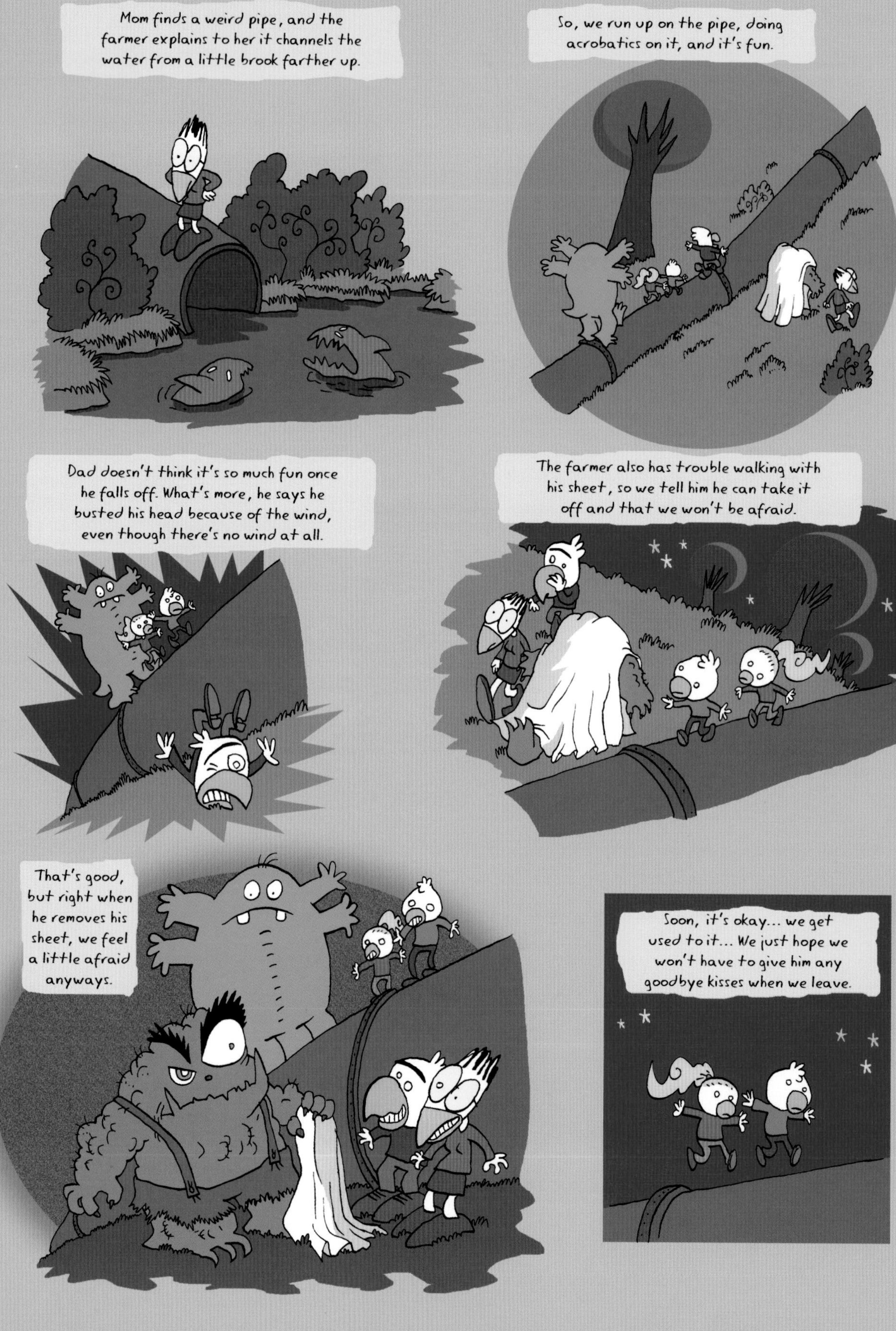
Mom finds a weird pipe, and the farmer explains to her it channels the water from a little brook farther up.
So, we run up on the pipe, doing acrobatics on it, and it's fun.
Dad doesn't think it's so much fun once he falls off. What's more, he says he busted his head because of the wind, even though there's no wind at all.
The farmer also has trouble walking with his sheet, so we tell him he can take it off and that we won't be afraid.
That's good, but right when he removes his sheet, we feel a little afraid anyways.
Soon, it's okay... we get used to it... We just hope we won't have to give him any goodbye kisses when we leave.

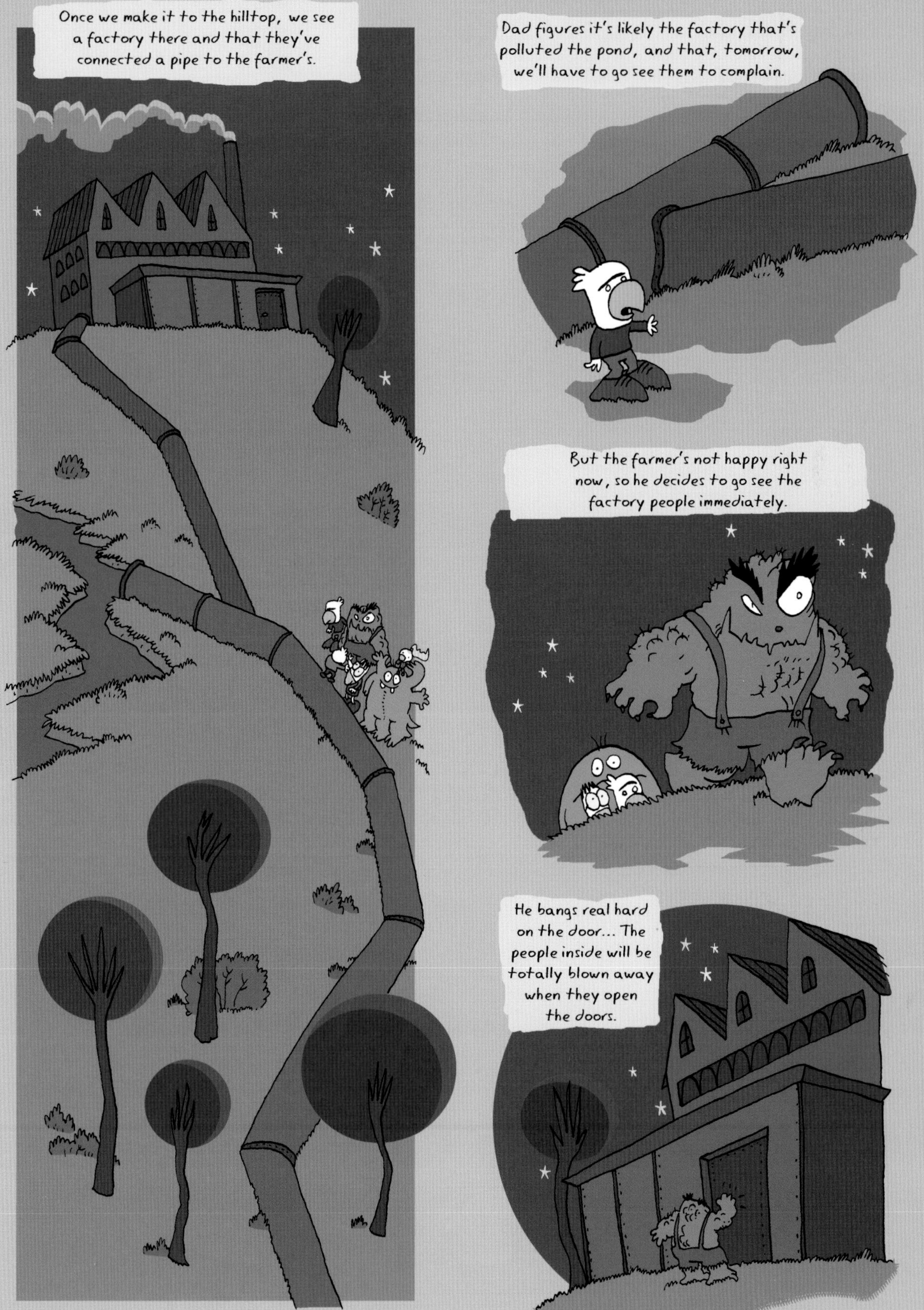
Once we make it to the hilltop, we see a factory there and that they've connected a pipe to the farmer's.
Dad figures it's likely the factory that's polluted the pond, and that, tomorrow, we'll have to go see them to complain.
But the farmer's not happy right now, so he decides to go see the factory people immediately.
He bangs real hard on the door... The people inside will be totally blown away when they open the doors.

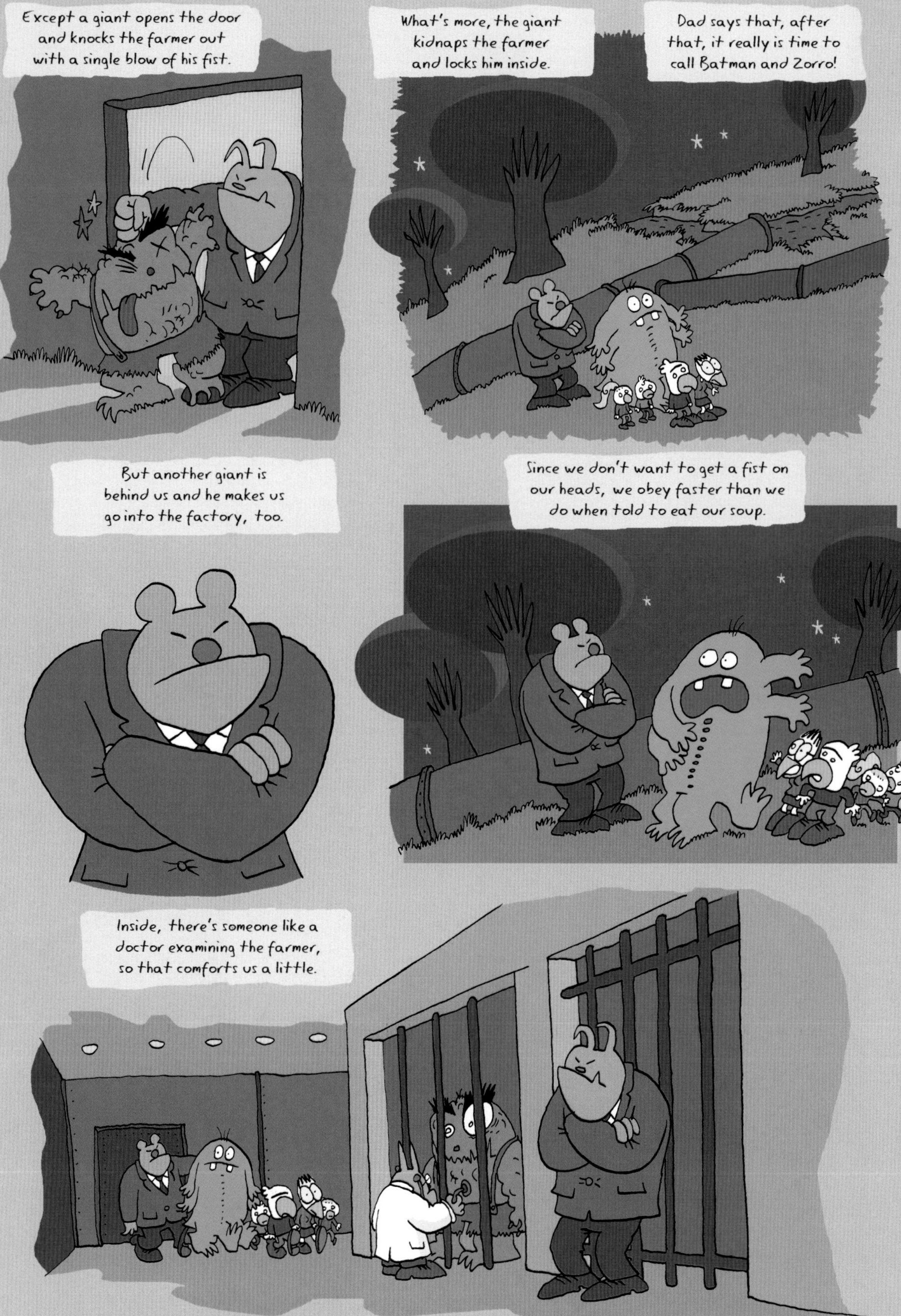
Except a giant opens the door and knocks the farmer out with a single blow of his fist.
What's more, the giant kidnaps the farmer and locks him inside.
Dad says that, after that, it really is time to call Batman and Zorro!
But another giant is behind us and he makes us go into the factory, too.
Since we don't want to get a fist on our heads, we obey faster than we do when told to eat our soup.
Inside, there's someone like a doctor examining the farmer, so that comforts us a little.

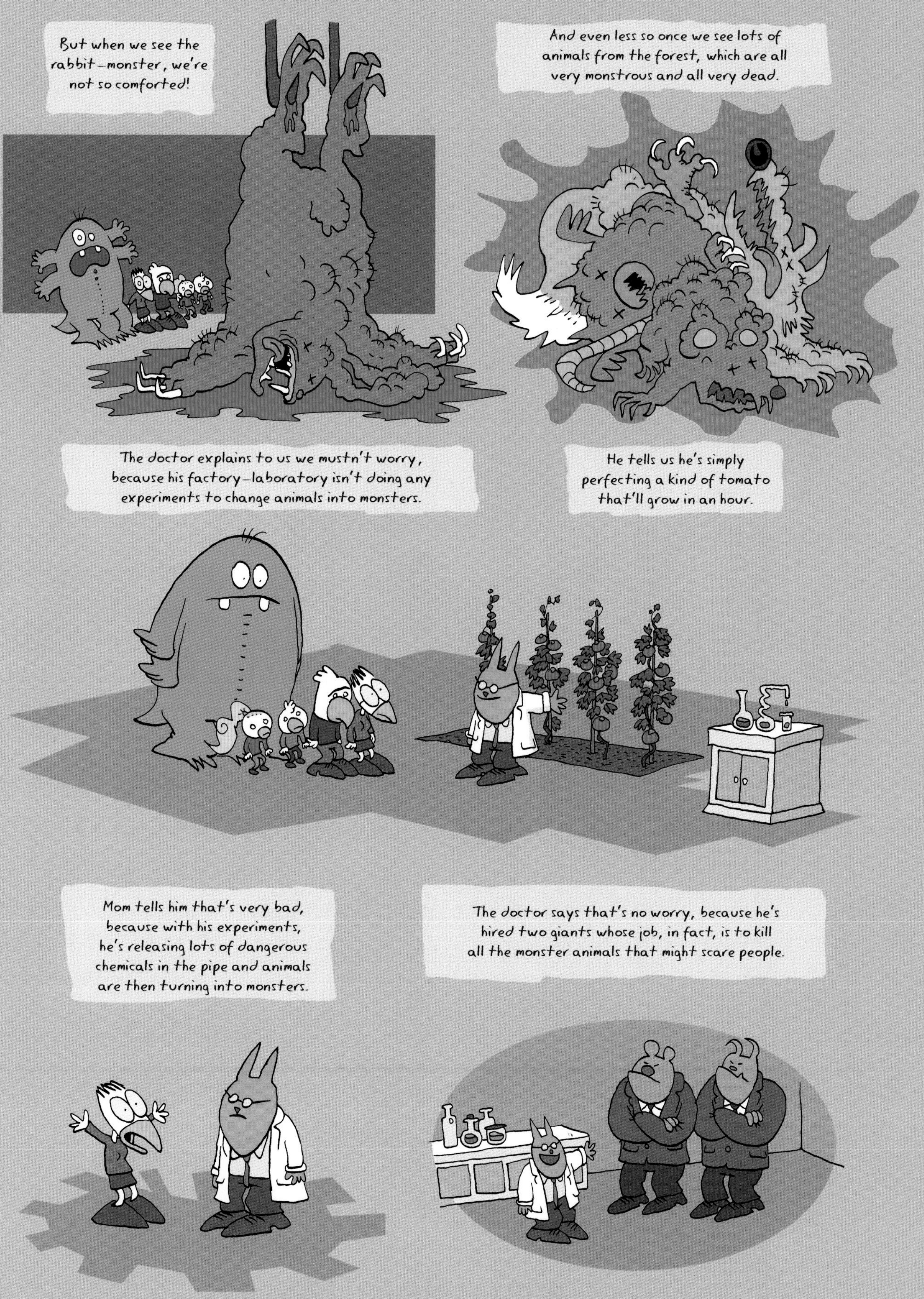
But when we see the rabbit-monster, we're not so comforted!
And even less so once we see lots of animals from the forest, which are all very monstrous and all very dead.
The doctor explains to us we mustn't worry, because his factory-laboratory isn't doing any experiments to change animals into monsters.
He tells us he's simply perfecting a kind of tomato that'll grow in an hour.
Mom tells him that's very bad, because with his experiments, he's releasing lots of dangerous chemicals in the pipe and animals are then turning into monsters.
The doctor says that's no worry, because he's hired two giants whose job, in fact, is to kill all the monster animals that might scare people.

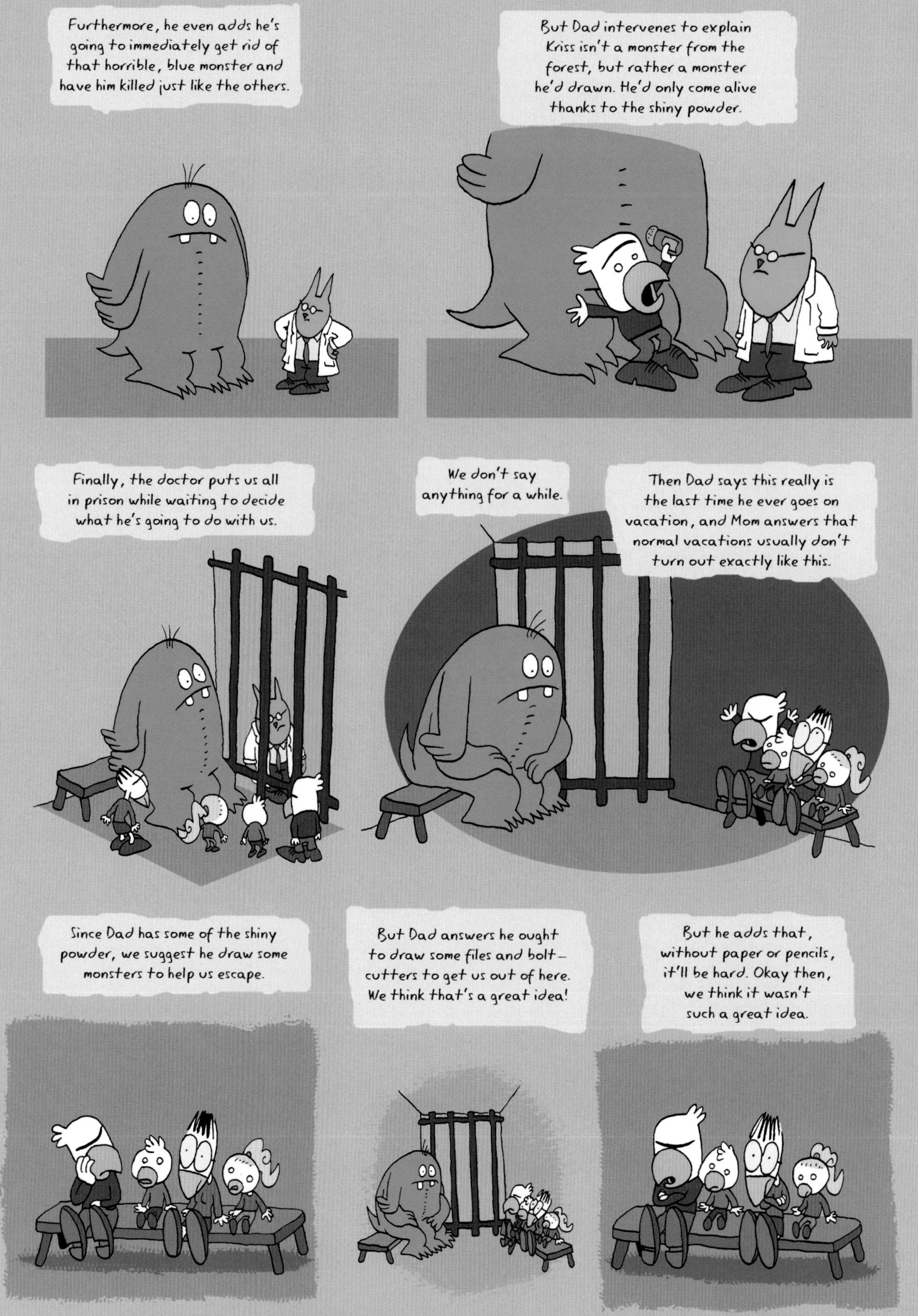
Furthermore, he even adds he's going to immediately get rid of that horrible, blue monster and have him killed just like the others.
But Dad intervenes to explain Kriss isn't a monster from the forest, but rather a monster he'd drawn. He'd only come alive thanks to the shiny powder.
Finally, the doctor puts us all in prison while waiting to decide what he's going to do with us.
We don't say anything for a while.
Then Dad says this really is the last time he ever goes on vacation, and Mom answers that normal vacations usually don't turn out exactly like this.
Since Dad has some of the shiny powder, we suggest he draw some monsters to help us escape.
But Dad answers he ought to draw some files and bolt-cutters to get us out of here. We think that's a great idea!
But he adds that, without paper or pencils, it'll be hard. Okay then, we think it wasn't such a great idea.

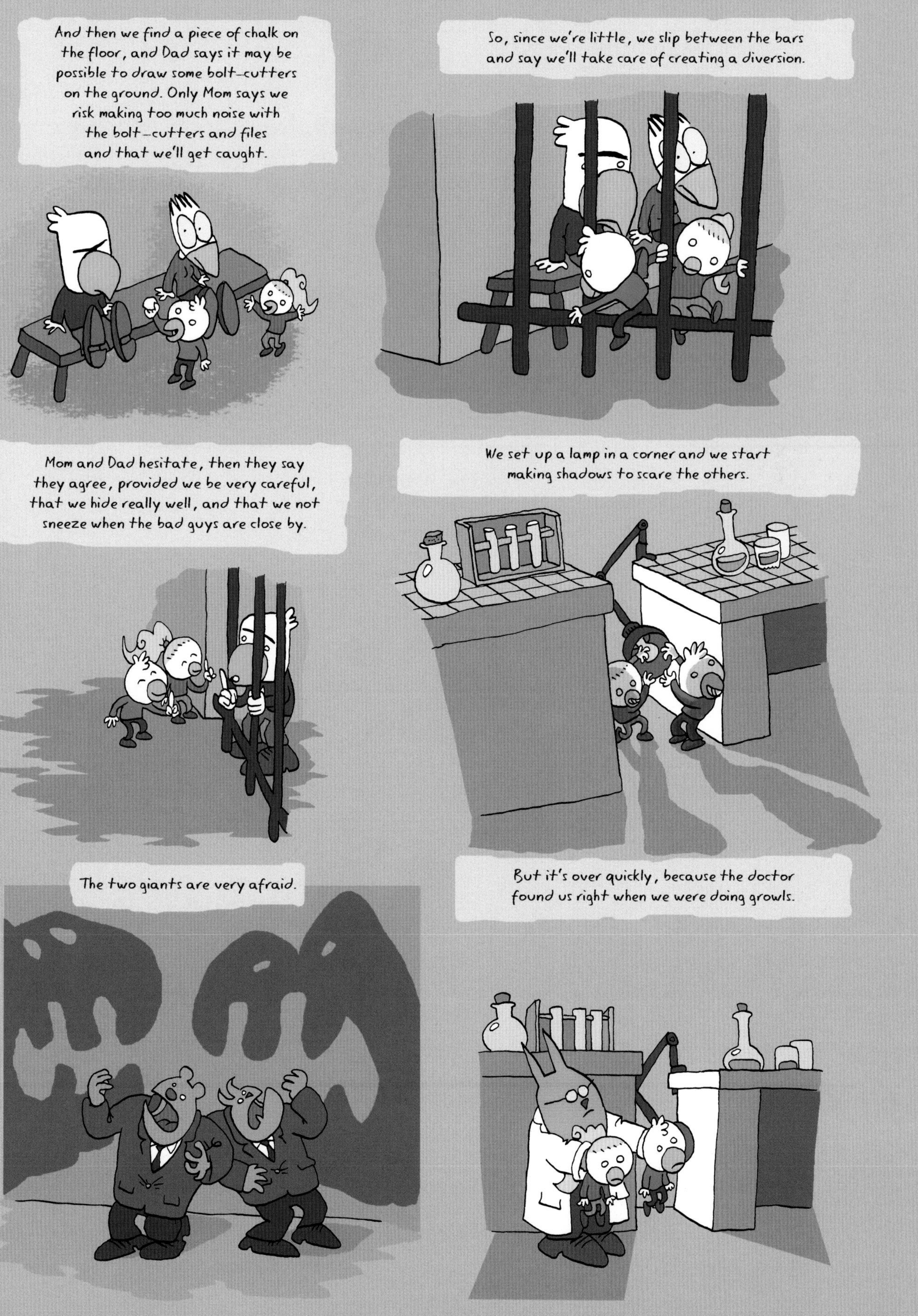
And then we find a piece of chalk on the floor, and Dad says it may be possible to draw some bolt-cutters on the ground. Only Mom says we risk making too much noise with the bolt-cutters and files and that we'll get caught.
So, since we're little, we slip between the bars and say we'll take care of creating a diversion.
Mom and Dad hesitate, then they say they agree, provided we be very careful, that we hide really well, and that we not sneeze when the bad guys are close by.
We set up a lamp in a corner and we start making shadows to scare the others.
The two giants are very afraid.
But it's over quickly, because the doctor found us right when we were doing growls.

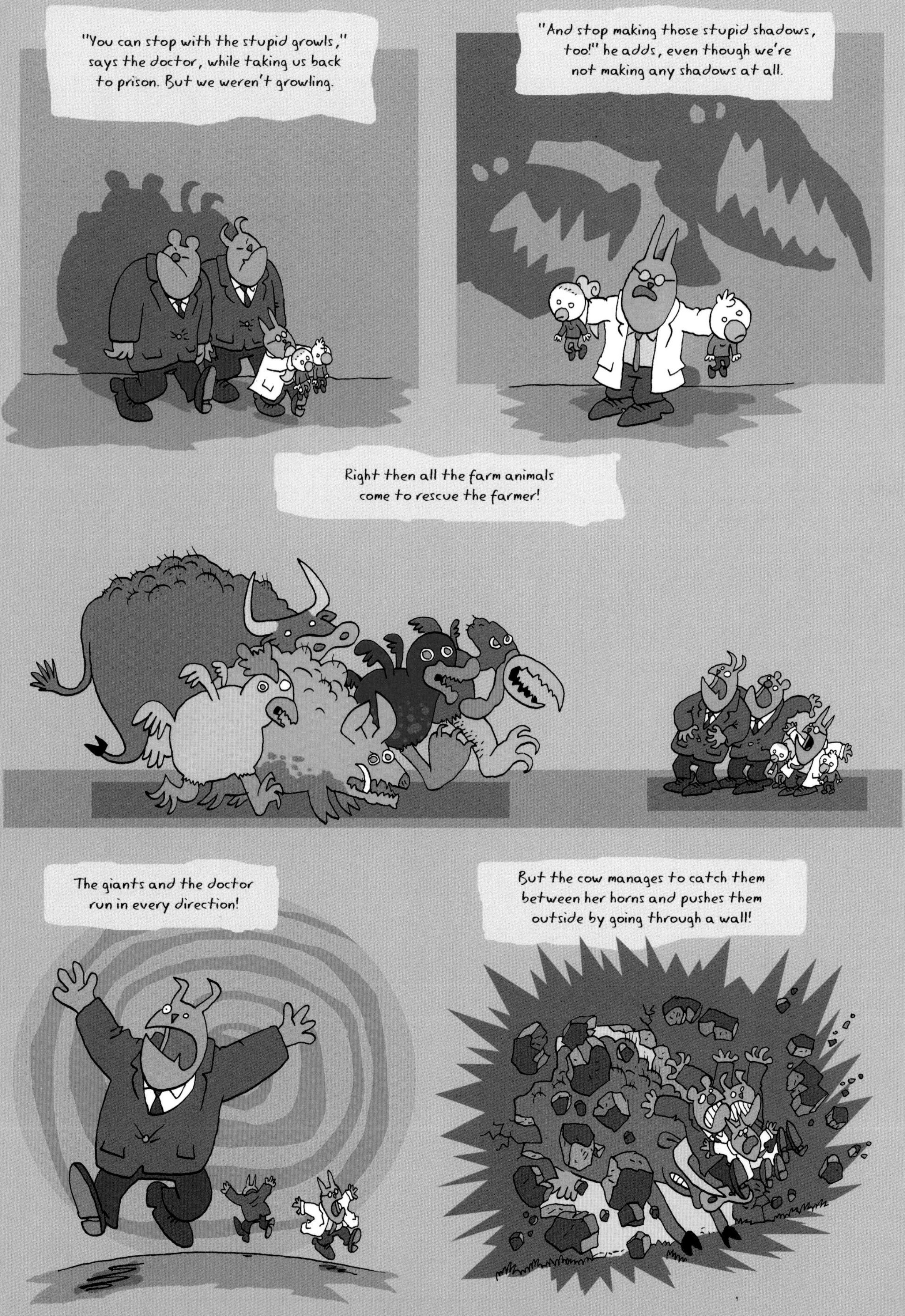
"You can stop with the stupid growls," says the doctor, while taking us back to prison. But we weren't growling.
"And stop making those stupid shadows, too!" he adds, even though we're not making any shadows at all.
Right then all the farm animals come to rescue the farmer!
The giants and the doctor run in every direction!
But the cow manages to catch them between her horns and pushes them outside by going through a wall!

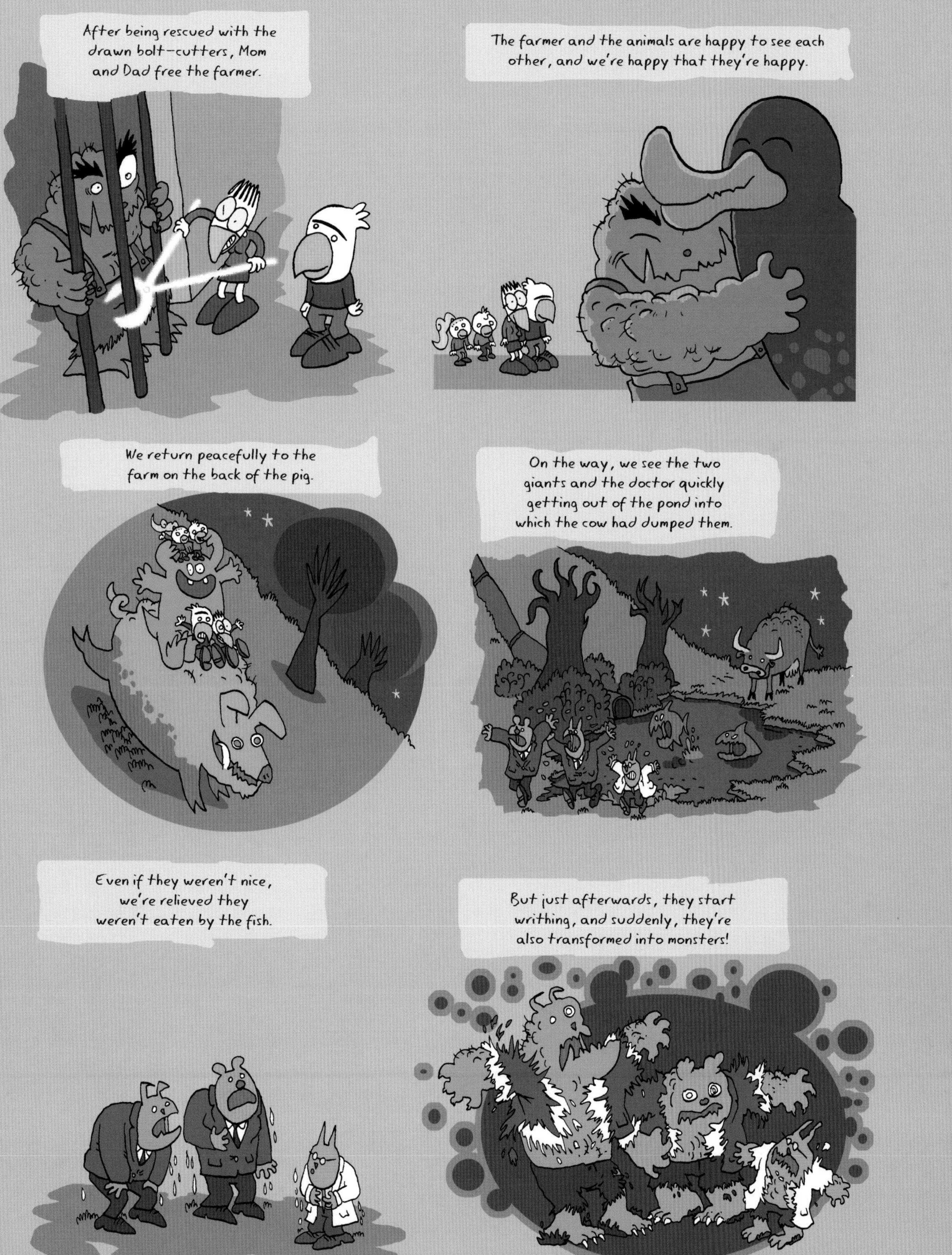
After being rescued with the drawn bolt-cutters, Mom and Dad free the farmer.
The farmer and the animals are happy to see each other, and we're happy that they're happy.
We return peacefully to the farm on the back of the pig.
On the way, we see the two giants and the doctor quickly getting out of the pond into which the cow had dumped them.
Even if they weren't nice, we're relieved they weren't eaten by the fish.
But just afterwards, they start writhing, and suddenly, they're also transformed into monsters!

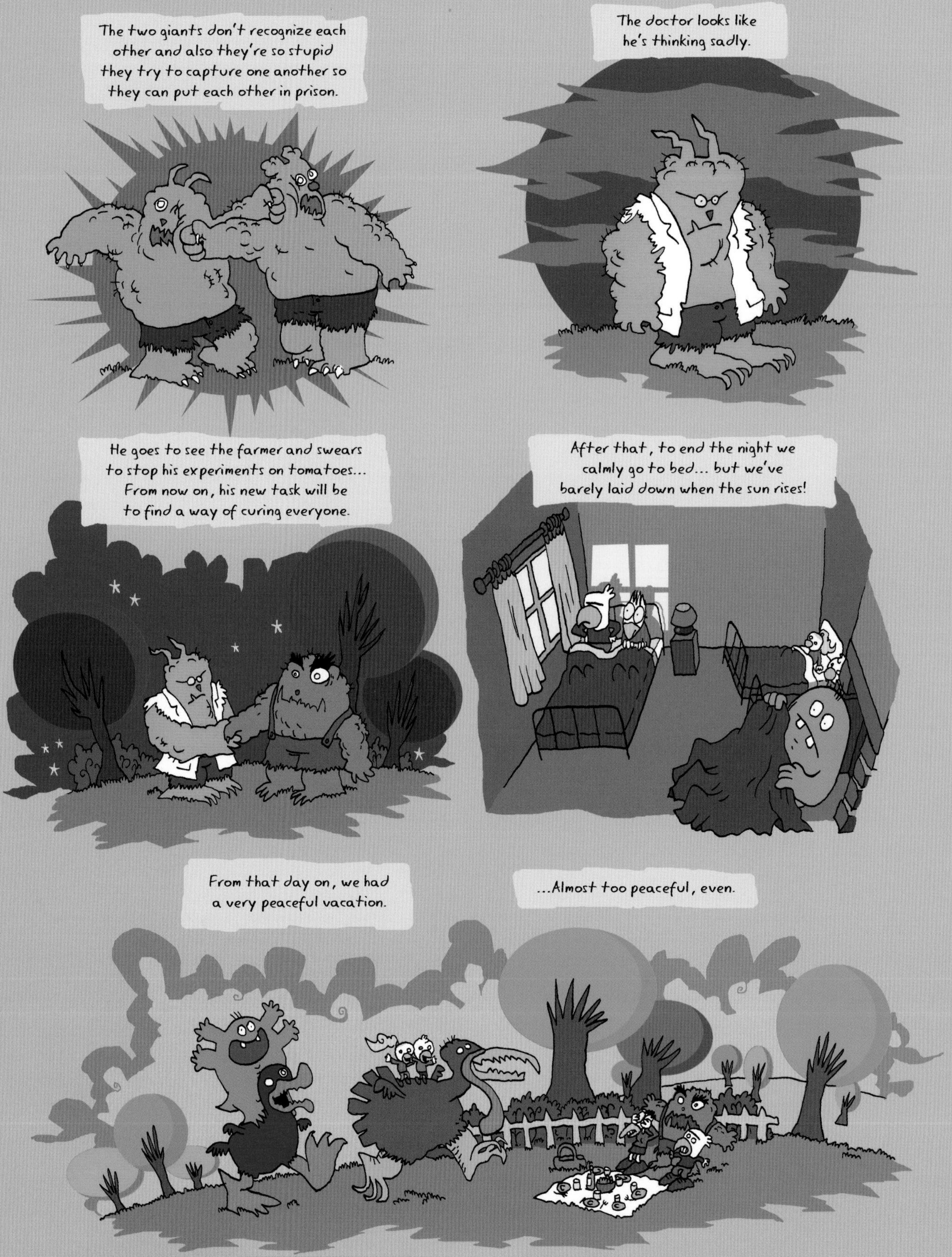
The two giants don't recognize each other and also they're so stupid they try to capture one another so they can put each other in prison.
The doctor looks like he's thinking sadly.
He goes to see the farmer and swears to stop his experiments on tomatoes... From now on, his new task will be to find a way of curing everyone.
After that, to end the night we calmly go to bed... but we've barely laid down when the sun rises!
From that day on, we had a very peaceful vacation.
...Almost too peaceful, even.

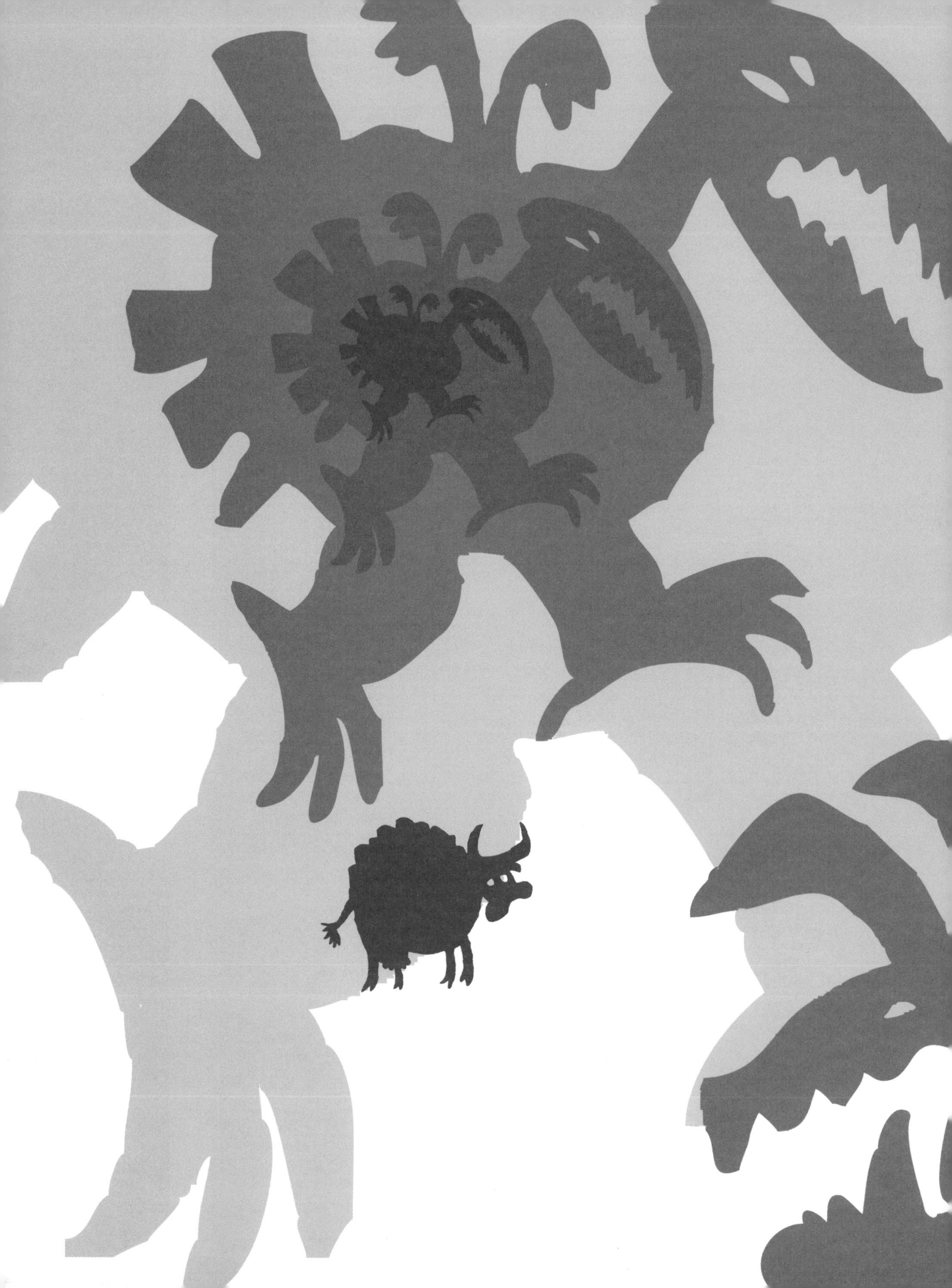